Wednesdays at Monti's

SUITE OF SHORT STORIES

June O. Underwood

ISBN: 979-8-9877907-5-5

Cover photo: June O Underwood
Design and layout by Anna Magruder

southeastmain.wordpress.com

Also by June O Underwood:

Sculpting the Mist: Reports from Elderhood 2019-2021

For Doris and Mary,

Who taught me most of what I know

about kinwork and storytelling

CONTENTS

HOME

Portland, Oregon, 2018

When V landed at the Portland airport, she called for an Uber and texted her family. Conrad, her husband of almost 60 years, and Caddie, their daughter, were confused. They assumed she was 3,000 miles away.

V had not stayed for the death. While V was breathing recycled plane air and flying over the Great Plains, Nora was drawing her last breaths at home, surrounded by the extended family in a room filled with cigarette smoke, stale beer smells, and sick-bed odors. Nora was dying at home, in the small Pennsylvania town where she had lived most of her adult life.

V was on her way to Oregon.

V had called Conrad and Caddie from Pennsylvania the night before her flight. She told them that Nora was very ill, and that Babs, Nora's daughter, was with her, and Bab's brothers with their kids were on their way. V did not mention her 4 a.m. flight.

Nora was V's cousin; she was also her friend, mentor, beloved. She died of brain cancer while V was looking at the snows swirling over Mount Hood.

V left Nora to face death alone.

Actually, V thought defensively, shifting around in her airline seat, Nora was not alone. Her descendants, the five children and their children and children's children, were now eating, drinking, and arguing, probably about the cost of the casket. V left them sleeping on the sick-room floor or in the junk-filled attic room.

It was, thought V, a babble, a chaos of people she scarcely knew. She had to go home. She had to breathe in the scent of the comforting firs in her little suburb. Home was quiet. Home smelled of coffee and herbal soaps. Home had big windows and no clutter. Home was in Oregon, far far away.

She had paid her respects, she told herself. She had spent time with Nora, sitting at her bedside. She had said her goodbyes. The clan had gathered, and now, even though she was the last of her generation, the putative matriarch, she was going home – back to Oregon.

V could hear Nora, in her nasal Appalachian accent, scolding, saying that she was forgetting her manners.

"Running away again," Nora would have said. "Always hiding from real life. All your fancy reading, and you can't even stay around for my funeral. You could have waited a couple of hours."

But then, another side of Nora also sneaked into V's imagining. Nora would say, had said, that funerals were for the living. Nora had said this at the other funerals V had actually flown to attend.

When V appeared in her black dress-up clothes, Nora would hug her, ask about Con and Caddie, tell her who else had died or was about to, and then would talk about the greening up of the Pennsylvania trees behind her house and how her geraniums and worm-eaten apples had done last year. Those funerals, of V's parents, Em and Eddie, as well as Nora's parents and one or two siblings and other cousins, were crowded affairs, full of relatives V didn't recognize. They involved wakes at bars as well as casseroles at local community centers. V was always asked by assorted semi-strangers about what it was like, out there with the Indians and Big Foot and long-haired hippies.

Nora's interest was in her people and so she took V through the family history – births, deaths, moves, divorces, sex changes and new partners – everything that happened since the last time she had seen her. V, drinking Nora's beer, listened and laughed, made appropriate faces and refrained from asking which side of the family and whose child Nora was talking about. It was enough that Nora thought that she, V, would know perfectly who Auntie Elkins was and why Brionne had to drop out of school. Nora's peopled world, her whole existence, was, for V, alive only when she, V, went back home to Pennsylvania.

And now V was fleeing that world, running away from the soft green hillsides, the crowded house, the labored breaths.

"Jesus Christ, Tiny," Nora would have said, "you could have waited 'till they shoveled the dirt over me." Nora, as she aged, forgot that V – for "Valentine" and even "Tiny" when V was small -- was now the brusque, wine-drinking adult. V was still Nora's little cousin who needed to be taught her manners.

"We'll need to send flowers – a lot of them – maybe a wreath," V said to Caddie as she dropped her flight bags inside the door. The living room where Conrad and Caddie waited for her felt empty and cold. A couch, a couple of chairs, paintings arranged singly on the walls. Even the vase of gladioli, brought by Caddie for Conrad, whom she was watching out for in V's absence, failed to bring V warmth.

"How was your trip, Mom?" asked Caddie.

Conrad kissed V on the cheek. "Welcome back," he said.

"Caddie, dial up the florist and order a large wreath for the funeral. Maybe something with reds and oranges. Babs and the family will be checking it out, so don't make it too exotic."

"I'll do it online, Mom. I'll get a good mix." Caddie picked up her phone and tapped into it.

Conrad reached to touch her. She drew in her arm.

Caddie reached for V's fingers. "Nora won't miss you at the cemetery. She'll have lots of others to boss around."

Conrad put his arm around V. "You probably want a bath, luv," he said. "There's left-over hummous and tabouli."

"I'll make you a gin-and-tonic, Mom, and you can drink it in the tub," said Caddie, finishing the florist order.

"You said your goodbyes," added Conrad, his arms now fully enveloping her.

V nodded and hid her face on Conrad's shoulder.

She had run away.

Iowa, 1974

In the past, Nora had often run toward V and her family, to help them out one way or another. When V was packing boxes for a move to another city for another university teaching job,

Nora and Babs had driven halfway across the country, from Pennsylvania to Iowa, to help her finish packing.

When they got there, they found a household silent with suppressed anger. Caddie, a sullen 15-year-old, resented losing her school and friends. Conrad was tight with worry and disgust – "Another move for your Mom's career!" he told Caddie.

V focused on her need to move. Her current job was ill-paid, and she was on a year-to-year contract. In Oregon, the pay was decent and she could teach Shakespeare and Virginia Woolf. And maybe do some painting. She had to get away from the small Iowa town where she couldn't wear shorts to the library or drink at the local tavern on Friday nights. She would go mad, she thought, if she had to stay in Iowa any longer. Caddie and Conrad would have to handle their own problems.

And then Nora and Babs showed up. They stayed a week. They slept on the floor on air mattresses. They boxed up books and wrapped china. They bought Chinese take-out and cooked dinners using Hamburger Helper. Nora bought Pepsi for herself and fresh coffee for Conrad and V. Caddie, a tenth grader, took Babs, a freshman in college, to the swimming pool. Conrad told Nora of his frustrations, and she listened and nodded. V packed her office things and told her colleagues of her frustrations, and they nodded and listened.

The last evening that Nora and Babs were with them in Iowa, Nora made a gingerbread cake in a frying pan. She made the two girls go out and buy whipping cream to top it, even as V explained, with annoyance, that the mixer had already been packed.

Nora put the cream into the only remaining unpacked bowl, grabbed a clean fork, and started churning "We'll each take a turn," she announced.

It took 45 minutes to whip the cream. Coating the cake with the soft curls, V said they'd use the rest in the next morning's coffee. Nora reminded her that she, Nora, only drank Pepsi. The two girls discussed whipped cream on Seven Up. The cake was declared a success.

After the dessert, the two young ones drifted into the empty living room where only the old piano sat, to be abandoned to new tenants. Caddie thrummed chords on it. The grown-ups cleaned up the dishes and put away the gingerbread –"for breakfast" Conrad said.

"With whipped cream" said V, suddenly feeling happy.

Babs called from the living room to Nora: "Mom, come here, look – it's that old church song book."

It was a battered Methodist hymnal, rescued years before from the little church where V and Nora had sung in the choir and where V and Conrad were married. The church had been torn down but V had kept the book.

Babs put the book on the piano. "Play it," she said to Caddie. Caddie started slowly through the chords and then added the melody with more confidence.

"I remember this song," Babs said. "Granny K always sang it when she got me dressed for church. Granny Em said Granny K couldn't carry a tune in a barrel."

It was a simple tune. Caddie played a phrase or two and then the two girls sang, their young sopranos blending. Nora moved into the front room, humming along. V stood at the kitchen door. Then in a strong alto, she joined them.

> *"I come to the garden alone / while the dew is still on the roses. / And the voice I hear, / sounding in my ear, / the son of God discloses.*

"And he walks with me and he talks with me"

V was suddenly walking up the dark country road to home, past the big cherry tree, keeping the ghosts away, singing to her 7-year-old self on an early spring evening. She could feel the light wind on her cheeks, and her heart racing a bit, and she sang louder. The country fields, full of rustling, dangerous skunks and panthers, surrounded her. She was all alone but able, through her voice, to keep the monsters at bay.

V's alto transposed into an upper range and soared.

> *"And he tells me I'm not alone. / And the joy we share as we tarry there/ None other has ever known."*

"Mom!" Caddie stopped playing. "How'd you do that? You aren't a soprano!"

V laughed.

"Your mom can do more than your pretty little head ever thought of," said Nora.

Caddie turned back to the piano. V sang the second verse from memory.

> *"He speaks and the sound of his voice / is so sweet the birds hush their singing. / And the melody that he gave to me / within my heart is ringing.*

The others joined in the chorus. Again V found herself soaring in high sweet harmony.

> *"And he walks with me*
> *And he talks with me*
> *And he tells me I am his own*
> *And the joy we share as we tarry there*
> *None other has ever known"*

"Wow," said Caddie to her mother. "I didn't know you could sing high harmony. Or that you knew any songs but Bob Dylan and Woodie Guthrie. And that *Traviata* drinking song."

"Don't forget Johnnie Cash," said Babs. "She and Mom could always belt out Johnnie Cash. *'How high's the water, Mama?'* "

"*Six feet high and risin*" sang V and Nora together.

The sing-along even pulled Conrad in, and the little family felt they could bear leaving the prairie town for the far west. It would be an adventure. They would write and tell Nora and Babs all about it.

When Nora got back to Pennsylvania, she was able to report to Em and Eddie, V's parents, that V and Caddie were doing just fine and that Conrad held his own with the two gals. And that V was drinking spendy coffee and that Caddie played the piano. And she (Nora) had to teach V that you didn't need a mixer to make whipped cream. Eddie laughed and said he knew his "Valkyrie," would be OK. Em laughed at Nora's descriptions of the frying pan gingerbread and the singing of the old songs. Eddie was glad that Conrad had checked the tires and wondered about the cost of the move.

Orrville, Pennsylvania, 1957

V and Nora had a history of helping one another. One long summer vacation when she was 17, V had stayed with Nora and her husband, RK, in the town up the road from Em and Eddie's. Nora was in her second pregnancy (she had five children altogether), having a difficult time of it, and Em sent V to help her. RK, who had gone to Texas to the oil fields, had returned to Orrville, complaining about crazy winds and rednecks. He found a job selling brushes and brooms while

Nora worked part-time downtown. V cooked, helped with the laundry, and babysat while RK slouched about the countryside, trying to convince farm women to buy mop-heads and dust cloths.

V didn't much like RK. He talked about himself all the time. Nora fought with him about spending her savings. During one weekend dinner, when V talked about Animal Farm and how some pigs are more equal than other pigs, he told her to stop showing off. When she stuck her tongue out at him, he wiped a butter knife across her nose. Nora, defending V, yelled at RK, picked up her plate, and threw it across the table into his lap. He loaded a fork with mashed potatoes and gravy and catapulted the mess onto her blouse.

V took the toddler outside, sat on the broken lawn chair, and listened to the yelling. Then RK came out and roared away, squealing his tires. Nora came out and sat down heavily on the steps.

"I guess it's time for you to go home." Nora eyed V sideways.

V nodded. Then she went inside and called her Mom, who said she would come and get her.

Laurelton, Pennsylvania, 1950

Nora, V, and RK had grown up in Laurelton, a tiny group of houses stuck between the Susquehanna River, the Pennsylvania Railroad tracks, and a northern ridge of the Appalachian Mountains. Laurelton had been a logging boomtown in the early 1900s but was now a hamlet of 60 people, the last dwellings before the county road left the river and went over Bellamy Mountain. Laurelton, ten miles from the nearest town of Orrville, consisted of patched-together housing and front yards cluttered with trucks up on blocks and stacks of old boards. It was a cluster of dirt-poor farming families and factory line workers, people just barely making it, set in their ways.

Eddie had steady work in town, so V and her siblings grew up in Em's untidy but well-loved household with clean and ironed clothes and roasts at least once a week. Nora's family was less well-off but still an economic cut above the shanty-housed kids.

Eddie was an enthusiastic reader of myth and history and when Em was too dopey from childbirth to stop him, had officially named the baby "Valentine." Em and the others shortened the name to "Val" or "Tiny," but when V learned to write her name, she became enchanted with how she could script an elegant "V."

"From now on," she announced to the assembled family at the supper table, "My name is V." And after that she refused to respond to anything else. When Em forgot and called for "Val" or "Tiny" to come set the table, V would go stone-still and silent until Em corrected herself.

V's mother, Em, and Nora's father were brother and sister, and the families had shared housing during the Depression. Both families remained in Laurelton during World War II, and both Nora and V had many siblings. Their respective households overflowed with down-on-luck friends and cousins who came for a week and remained for a year. Em stayed home with the kids (V and three older brothers) while Eddie worked in a ball-bearing factory across the river. Nora's waitress mother and her steelworker father both worked in Orrville. During long summer vacations, Nora's older brothers were in charge of her. They were, as Nora put it, "a pain in the patootie." The kids fought constantly, so Em suggested that Nora come and stay with V and her family. Nora became Em's best helper.

Em taught Nora and Nora taught V to use the wringer washing machine in the basement. Em warned Nora to watch 7-year-old V carefully, to make sure she didn't catch her braids in the wringer. The girls hung underwear on the lines hidden by sheets and towels and diapers, so the neighbors wouldn't gossip. Supper duties included 10-year-old Nora supervising V in cutting the eyes out of potatoes that Nora peeled. Nora snapped at V for not drying cups carefully on the bottom ridges, and V sometimes had to go outside by herself to stomp off the anger that Nora's bossiness provoked.

But often the summertime chores were light, and Nora and V could go off by themselves – "Young Ladies' Adventures" Em called them. Em had a special fondness for her girls.

When she was a toddler, V went with Em to pick wild strawberries and dandelion greens, and Em showed her where to find huckleberries and teaberries. Later, V explored on her own, up the mountain and through the river bottoms. V loved the swampy mysteries of the bottoms and the pine trees on the hills. She spent hours roaming, by herself, through the cedars and maples and dogwood. She felt she owned hidden towering fir trees and the muddy hideouts underneath where no one, she was sure, had ever been.

V, after long thought, decided to show Nora her special summer place, the violet grove that belonged to V alone. She had learned through her reading that her summer place was a "grove," a "flowered glade," and she knew that in the cool June days, it would be spread with sweet violets – johnny jump-ups. They were her favorites.

So one June day, V announced to her mother that she and Nora were going for a hike.

Em waved her hand, "Be back in time for supper," she said and returned to cooing over a squalling toddler. Em was easy with the girls, glad that V and Nora got along so well.

V snuck a box of crackers into her bag: "We'll find some berries up the hill," she told Nora.

V led the way through the brush, going up a faint trail that ended at the Pennsy railroad tracks. Across the tracks was a strip of jimson weeds, elderberry bushes and chokecherry trees. The half-dead underbrush was thick and whipped at their faces. They slid down to a swampy hollow where skunk cabbage blooms lay rotting.

"Watch out for the skunk leaves – they sting." V nodded toward the big leafy foliage along the slimy edges of the hollow.

They jumped over the swamp bottom, skidding on its mud. Nora grunted "Ugh," and V grinned at her. They moved through tall ferns, laurel bushes, and scrubby second growth, dogwood and redbud that Eddie called "trash," and V used to decorate her hideaways.

As they climbed higher up the mountain, the trees became larger and the light dimmed. Hemlock and pine, along with an occasional birch, caught the sun above their heads. The forest floor here was easy to walk through, interrupted only by a fallen log or the odd mountain laurel. Wood anemone and trout lilies peeped out from downed tree branches. Trailing pine popped up through the littered forest floor. The girls kicked up last fall's leaves, which made fine rustling noises as they swished them.

"Where are we?" Nora was becoming impatient.

"Shhh. We're almost there."

The forest lightened and then opened out into a large bright meadow. The girls stopped, dazzled by the sun-strewn space. Penstemon and Jacob's ladder edged into the dim woods. Lilies of the valley, wild lupine, bellflower, and deep purple and yellow violets filled the meadow. Meadow grasses, heated in the sun's warmth, scented the air. The girls' feet sank into green moss at the forest's edge. Their footsteps made no sound.

The girls picked a mossy spot warmed by the sun and plopped down. V picked two violets and handed one to Nora, showing her that they could eat the flower heads and then chew the stems.

The two of them lay back on the moss and stared at the bits of cerulean blue sky framed by forest green leaves. They squinted, finding shapes in the clouds. Their eyes drooped; the warm earth made them sleepy.

"My back itches," announced Nora, squirming with sudden restlessness.

"It's probably ants."

They squealed and jumped up.

Shaking out their blouses, the two hiked across the big clearing. V told Nora it was a "violet grove" and that it was special and secret, and that she daren't tell anybody. Nora promised, licked her right finger, and crossed it along the palm of V's left hand to seal her pledge. They climbed up the hill beyond the grove. V doled out crackers, and the two used their tongues to scoop up the crumbs from their hands. They found a birch tree, and stripped off a few lower twigs, which V announced would provide them with liquid. It was too early for huckleberries, but there were a few teaberries and lots of leaves to chew on. The trail home, which ran close to the paved mountain road, was wider and smoother, and the girls ran downhill, squealing as they tumbled over roots.

Laurelton, Pennsylvania, 1950s

Visiting the violet grove became a summer ritual. Lying on the cool moss, the girls studied the clouds for omens. They found kittens and whales and big-nosed faces. Side-by-side they lay, basking in the sun and silence and soothing mossiness. Then, one or the other would giggle or sniff or sneeze, and they would jump up and head back into the woods to the trail home. Once they took Em with them and she was enchanted, mentioning it often over the years.

The grove with its rituals was almost violated when Bobby Kirkman, Booby-Bobby, trailed them up the mountain. Bobby was clumsy, unable to move through bushes silently, and the girls always heard him as he followed them, ducking behind trees. They led him through burdock and nettle-strewn meadows, pretending they didn't know he was there. Finally, one August afternoon, they let him catch up. The game changed to cowboys and Indians, ambushing each other from behind bushes and trees. But the girls never allowed Booby-Bobby to visit the violet grove.

A few years later, Bobby and his parents moved to Philly. In the city Bobby grew thinner, and when he visited his grandparents, who still lived in Laurelton, V refused to play with him. She told Nora he was nasty. He bullied the younger kids. He bragged that he had girlfriends who "taught him things." He showed off his fancy sneakers and tight pants and his new skinny body.

As the summers went on, the trips to the Grove lessened. Nora became sharp-tongued and defiant. She was attractive, lithe, funny and full of imagination. Bobby, now Robert Kirkman the third, better known as RK, stayed with his grandparents during the summer and became part of the older crowd. V was left to wander alone in the woods. The big kids spent their days stealing apples and swimming in the river. River swimming was strictly forbidden, so they had to sneak off without bathing suits. V sometimes watched them from up the mountain.

During the summer that Em was hospitalized with pneumonia, Eddie put Nora, then 17, in charge, while he worked and spent evenings with Em. Then Em was sent to a sanitorium to recuperate. V was told to do whatever Nora said, and the two of them fumbled their way through the next couple of months.

Nora was crazy busy, desperate to keep up with the feeding and cleaning chores. She made breakfast and lunch for the family and the girls peeled the 10 or 12 potatoes for supper. The house needed swept, the floors mopped and the beds changed weekly. The pile of dirty dishes was unending. Everyone dressed in freshly washed and ironed clothes for Sunday school and church. V and Nora, in starchy choir robes, sang for the adult services.

Nora fought with her brothers, who hung out at the house, and was impatient with V. Nora sometimes left V with the baby and joined the older boys for a smoke or a quick skinny dip. V resented being left behind, but she always did what Nora told her.

And when she could, V sneaked away from Nora's bossiness and the chaotic household, hiding in the tiny church on the hill. There it was quiet and cool. Sunlight from the two high arched windows spread rainbows across the pews. V found the colors, named, in the World Book Encyclopedia. She memorized them to recite to herself on her next church visit. Nora sniffed at V's research but didn't mention her absences from the noisy cluttered house.

Neither of the girls got to the violet grove that summer.

Laurelton, Orrville, and State College, Pennsylvania, late 1950s, mid-1960s

Then Nora was 18, out of high school, working in a beauty salon across the river, and RK came back to live full time with his grandparents in Laurelton. Old Mrs. Kirkman doted on her grandson and Grandpa Kirkman tolerated him, even though "Fella can't even change a tire."

And Nora took up with RK. "Took up" was the way she put it – he was not, she insisted, her boyfriend. RK had wrangled an old Chevy out of his grandparents, and he and Nora souped it up. Nora was good at fixing cars – changing spark plugs, working on the timing -- better than RK. But RK could get beer, and the two of them found hidden places to park and drink in secret. They stayed out until 3 a.m., and Aunt Em warned Nora about things that happened to girls who came home smelling of beer. Eddie disapproved of the way RK treated cars.

Nora kept on with RK because, she said, he had money, was fun to hang out with, and they could both talk about their awful families. Finally, of course, RK knocked her up, and they married.

RK, bored with Pennsylvania, took a job in the Texas oil fields, and Nora, pregnant, stayed behind, moving in with V's family.

She shared V's bed and worked part-time at the country store on the road to town. She and V laughed slyly at Nora's tales of burly farmhands looking for underwear for their wives' birthdays. As she grew larger in her pregnancy, Nora stayed home more, helping Em with the housework, and sewing baby clothes. Nora listened to V's summaries of novels she was reading. RK's absence was a relief for Nora: "He wasn't much interested," she told V, "in anything other than my big, baby-coming boobs, which is," she said, rolling her eyes, "so boorrrrring."

Then, Nora and RK were parents. RK left the oil fields. RK's grandparents bought a house for them in Orrville, 10 miles from Laurelton. Nora had four more kids.

After Babs, the last of the five siblings and the only daughter, was born, Nora got her tubes tied. She became more and more unhappy with RK, who traveled a lot for jobs he got fired from. Nora held the family together, acting as the primary money earner. She eventually found work at a local factory. She was good at mechanics and flirting, and men liked her. RK overheard the guys talking, got drunk, and threatened Nora, not for the first time. She picked up a frying pan and told him "You have to sleep sometime!" V admired Nora's way of stopping a bully. When RK disappeared for good, Nora stayed put, raising the children by herself.

V graduated in the academic track in high school and became the first in her family to go to college. She loved it. The college library was quiet with tall arched windows, full of books and ideas. The dorm food was nice and bland and there were no dishes to wash. She could go home as often as she wanted and see Em and Eddie and her brothers' kids.

State College, Pennsylvania, 1965

After V got her undergraduate degree in English and studio art, she and Conrad, who had graduated a year before, married, remaining in the college town while V worked on her masters' degree. Em and Eddie were proud of her, even as they wondered what she would do with an English degree. A painting minor was even less useful. But V had Conrad who could earn a living, so they didn't worry too much.

Nora and her current friend ("Not a boyfriend and not a stay-over either," she insisted), helped V and Conrad paint the little house they rented near campus. The painting party was wild–even the rickety wooden furniture became hot pink. V had a grand time. She and Conrad danced to "Smoke Gets in Your Eyes" and then she jitter-bugged with Nora's friend and felt young and sexy. Nora and her friend left at 3 AM, after kisses all around, which V found naughty and wonderful.

She also woke up sick the next morning, the first time she had ever had a hangover, which turned out not to be a hangover but morning sickness. Baby Caddie was born in the hospital where Em had had all her babies, but it was Nora, weeks later, who found V sitting in an old pink rocker, sobbing, baby wet and whimpering in her arms. The Odyssey, an assignment for her classical lit seminar, lay on the floor beside them.

Nora put down her pocket book and took baby Caddie away from V. She snuggled the child against her coat, and V went to the bathroom. She could hear Nora humming an old hymn to Caddie, whose crying had stopped.

V peed and washed her face and then soaped her hands, over and over. She found a dry shirt, one with only a little spit-up on it. When she came out, she put the kettle on to boil.

Nora came out of the bedroom, holding Caddie in a dry diaper and shirt. The baby lay quiet against Nora's shoulder. V raised her arms to take the baby.

"Had any coffee yet?" Nora eyed V without offering Caddie.

V shook her head; her lips trembled.

"Conrad was late for work and baby wouldn't stop crying. I fed her but she wouldn't stop crying."

"Have some coffee." Nora's brusque tone was comforting.

Nora held the baby. V poured hot water into a couple of cracked cups and put instant coffee into her own. Nora put her hand over the top of her cup. She didn't drink coffee – she had told V it was a college-kid's brew. She preferred Pepsi. V sat down and blew on the coffee, cooling it.

"Some eggs?" Nora got up and opened the refrigerator door, holding the baby snug against her body.

V's voice rose through her snot: "No!" And then, more calmly, "No, we need them. For dinner. Payday's not 'til Friday."

"Oh for God's sake," said Nora. She stood quiet for a minute. "I got some groceries in the car. Here – have a kid."

And handing over the baby, Nora went out into the snow and brought in her own week's groceries.

V, clutching the now-sleeping baby, protested, but Nora ignored her, putting the boxes of Kraft Mac-and-Cheese into the cupboards and potatoes into the fridge. She even stowed a dozen eggs alongside the two in the egg compartment. Baby Caddie slept on in V's arms.

"Why didn't you say something?" demanded Nora.

"I didn't want to. And Conrad's parents would find out and you know how they are.

"And I have a test in classics next week and I need it to finish and I have to – did you know I got that job in West Virginia? Conrad can quit the bookstore and the money is pretty good. We just have to make it 'til I get my degree. And we don't have much stuff to move."

"Actually," her face changed a bit, "we don't have anything to move – even Caddie sleeps in the landlord's dresser."

The thought of the landlord's hot-pink chest of drawers brought on the first giggles. V knew they would make it just fine if she could just get through the Odyssey test. And keep Caddie from crying when Conrad needed sleep.

After Nora had changed V and Conrad's bed – at least, V thought, there were clean sheets – Nora made oatmeal that she doctored with some stiff honey. She slapped it down in front of V.

"Eat" she said. "I gotta run."

Laurelton, Pennsylvania, 1969

V finished her master's degree and then she and Conrad and Caddie moved to West Virginia. In the following years, V found other college jobs, going west to Ohio and Indiana, further from her family, until she got tired of teaching freshman comp and was granted a Penn State assistantship that required teaching freshman while she worked on her PhD. Conrad became a journalist, reporting on the planning and zoning board, high school basketball, and college campus riots. At Penn State, V and Conrad and Caddie moved into university housing. The apartment felt familiar, stained rugs, a tiny refrigerator, and baby-shit green walls.

V and Conrad and Caddie went back to Em and Eddie's often during V's PhD years. Home meant free food and comfortable beds and relatives who doted on Caddie. But the family visits were not altogether comfortable. Nora made sarcastic remarks about V's education. Em and Eddie were traditional Republicans, pro-Nixon. They watched TV after supper and saw chaos and violence. Anti-war rock throwing, Black Power sit-ins, sex, drugs, and rock-n-roll. More than once, the post-supper story-telling became battles over student behavior.

"They could just cover up their big fat asses," said Nora, one Friday night after supper. V, Caddie, and Conrad were home from State College, and Nora was there with her kids.

"Ignorant brats!" said Nora, talking about college students. "If they paid more attention to their studies and less to their undies, the country might amount to something."

"Who is this "they?" demanded V. "I'm a student and I pay a lot of attention to my work. And I don't show my underwear."

"Now wait a minute." Nora said. "Jesus Christ, V, I watch more news than you do with all your books and notes and fancy classes. Dammit, the language, they use…."

"Oh, for heaven's sake. You swear more than anyone I know," said V.

"Goddamit V, you know what I mean. I mean that "F" word and calling the cops pigs."

The argument went on. Conrad and Eddie went out the front door to examine the lawn mower. The kids drifted out to the back yard and a badminton game.

Em put her coffee cup down hard and said, "Not at the dinner table."

"It's after dinner," said V, still glaring at Nora. "And Nora thinks it's all right to kill Vietnamese babies but just can't stand one nasty word. Well, 'baby killer,' that's a bit more nasty."

Em stood up. "That's enough," she said. She took Caddie out to join Eddie and Conrad. Nora and V stood up and started clearing the table. They carried the dirty dishes to the sink and washed and dried them. They put away the remains of the roast. They did not speak.

Then Nora said, "Jesus Christ, V, you sound just like a fancy-pants S.O.B. on TV."

"And you sound just like those slobbering greasy rednecks on TV," said V, and grinned back.

After a bit Nora said, "Well, I did hem my purple skirt the other day. I was starting to look like an old granny."

And V said, "Yeah, and I have taken to wearing long hippie skirts when I'm teaching. If I teach in my regular short skirts and turn my back to write on the black board, I can hear the snickers before I even get my arms raised."

The two women grabbed beers and went out on the porch to join Em and Caddie.

Portland, Oregon, Orrville and Laurelton, Pennsylvania, 1980s

V finished her PhD and then she, Conrad, and Caddie moved west again, to a small college in Iowa. Conrad worked at the local paper, covering pothole complaints and the school board while V taught freshman and sophomores and did a little art on the side. It was an OK job, but when she got an offer from

Portland State in Oregon, she was relieved. A big campus could offer up more liberal friends. And Portland sounded like a change from small college towns – a city to explore.

V, Conrad, and Caddie moved to the Pacific Northwest, 3,000 miles from home. The family back in Pennsylvania grew up, married, and expanded with more grandbabies. Caddie got an engineering degree from MIT and looked for jobs near her parents. V liked her new job, and she and Conrad seldom found time to go back east. V and Nora spoke on the phone a couple of times a year. V, when she talked to Nora, would slip into Nora's nasal twang. But V's chats had become full of "big" words, words too big for Nora to tolerate. She would get sharp tongued and remind V of "where you came from, baby."

V bit her tongue; she felt guilty about moving far away and loving the roads along the slopes of ancient volcanoes and alongside the Pacific Ocean. She reveled in her lovely house and the well-paid job that allowed her to deal with books and ideas. Nora became a person of legend, of dining-out stories, and distant in V's thoughts.

Nora's boys joined the armed services, married, and set up their own homes. Babs went to the teacher's college in Orrville and never married. One by one, Orrville's factories closed, including the one where Nora worked. Nora's dyslexia made jobs hard to get and harder to keep. She worked as a house cleaner, gradually morphing into the person who was called to "help out" when grandma or grandpa got cancer. She earned her certificate as a home health aid. She bought large exotic birds that she housed in her living room. Her house, small rooms and little windows, became crowded with "stuff." She couldn't throw out the magazines that she loved thumbing through. She loved tourist souvenirs, saucers with "Welcome to Tampa" in neon green and plates touting "Big Wonderful Wyoming." She kept vases into which she dropped labeled keychains – Dallas and Chicago – and magnets for the fridge. She went to garage sales for entertainment.

"Never know when you might need a crowbar," she'd say, when she found one for a nickel. She kept pots of geraniums on her front steps whose boards were sagging and bouncy.

Then Em came down with Alzheimer's. "Came down with" was the euphemism they used. Eddie took care of her, even as she lost track of where she was and started roaming. Nora quit her nurse's-aid job and moved in to help the elders.

When Eddie died, V and Conrad flew to Pennsylvania for the funeral. Afterward Conrad went back to Oregon, while V, having the summer off to do research, stuck around the old Laurelton home. Reinserted into family, she agreed to stay with Em for a few weeks so Nora could go home and rest up.

When Nora showed up at the old house a few days later, she saw the back door swinging open and two figures, V and Em, walking down the road toward the mountain.

V was pleading with Em. "Mama, you are home. Home is this way; back here, back up the road. Come on, let's go back."

Em marched forward. She was skinny and strong. She shook off V's tug. "I want to go home" she said. She would not turn back. Nora pulled the car a bit beyond them and got out. V looked at her, big eyed and desperate.

"She won't come back. I can't stop her."

Em went past Nora's car and then cut through the roadside weeds to a faint trail toward the railroad track and the mountain beyond.

"I'm going home," she said.

Nora held up her hand at V, warning her to stay back.

"Hey Em, where ya goin'?" Nora called.

"I'm going home. I want to go home." Em said as she stumbled up the trail.

"Here, come on and jump in. I'll drive you." Nora turned back to the car. After a minute, Em turned around and came back down.

"I want to go home" she said to Nora.

"Oh," said Nora, walking around and opening the passenger door. "You want to go home. Come on. Hop in. Up the mountain we will go. We'll drive you. Drive you home."

Em came back and got into the car. Nora returned to the driver's seat and V got in the back.

"Lock her door," said Nora quietly.

V reached forward and pushed down the lock.

Nora drove across the tracks. Em settled in her seat. A short distance up the mountain, Nora pulled off the road. "There's the lane home, Auntie Em."

V unlocked the door, Em got out and waited for the two of them, and they went up the trail to the grove, smaller now with new tree encroachments, but still paved with moss and violets.

"I'm tired," said Nora, and sat down on a mossy patch.

"Me too," said Em. And she and V joined Nora. The three women lay back on the moss and looked at the clouds. V called them pillows and elephants and Em listened. Finally,

Nora said she was feeling ants in her pants, and Em laughed and they got up, brushed themselves off, and walked back to the car.

Em said happily, "A Ladies' Adventure." Nora and V laughed along with her. Nora took them back down the road, across the tracks to home, where V and Em drank cold coffee and thumbed through an album of family photos. Nora made dinner for the two of them and left, without eating, to take care of her own chores.

Not too long after that, Em went into a nursing home. When Em died, V flew back for the funeral. Neither she nor Nora went to the violet grove.

Orrville, Pennsylvania, 2016

Nora lived the rest of her life in her dilapidated house in town. Her big tropical birds screamed and screeched when she talked to V on the phone. Nora never re-married ("never gonna pick up dirty socks again") and started to call V every Sunday. She told V about the old guys she, Nora, nursed and how they tried to pinch her bottom. She complained that her furnace died and the guy who repaired it must have gone to Florida on what she paid. She listed the goodies she found at that Saturday's garage sale and the way the old folks whose kids were having the sale had kept every goddamn plastic dish they ever had and even an old chamber pot, but that she, Nora, "found some real goodies among the trash."

"Jesus Christ, V," Nora sputtered, "You wouldn't believe what people have in their houses. It's really something."

V laughed and told Nora about her gardens and neighborhood walks and what Caddie was doing. She didn't mention her paintings, which were on exhibit at a local gallery, nor Conrad's work on Wikipedia.

V and Conrad, when V retired, had found an open, airy house in an old Portland suburb. Caddie got a job with the Portland city government, living near her parents. When V flew back to Pennsylvania for her youngest niece's wedding, she spent a lot of time on Nora's back porch, laughing about old times and catching up on stories about the family genealogy and where Aunt Mabel was buried.

At one point in that visit, Nora's entire family and some of V's siblings were gathered at a picnic table in Nora's weedy front yard, eating chips and drinking beer.

"Well you know that black guy wasn't born in the United States and isn't even a citizen. He doesn't even have an American name." Nora's voice came from the other end of the table.

V stopped what she was saying. "Nora, what in the world are you talking about? That's just stupid lies. Nonsense. Made up by a pussy grabber."

"Watch your tongue," said Nora defiantly. "This is my house."

"Your house, your schmouse. It's just, just slander, all lies." V was suddenly furious.

Until this moment during V's visit, the family had avoided politics. Most of them didn't vote. They all knew V was an old hippie protester; they all knew Nora watched too much TV and had "opinions." The clan, arranged down each side of the table, sat, quite still.

"Goddammit, this is the United States of America and I can say whatever I damn well please." Nora was loud, insistent.

"And I can get up and walk away any time I damn well please," yelled V.

Neither of the women moved.

Finally, one of the sisters-in-law asked another how she got her tuna casserole so crunchy and a nephew took up the question of the best tire place in town. V sat for a while and then excused herself. She went into the house and out the back door and walked around Nora's garden. She lifted a raspberry from the vine, thinking of smashing it. Then she ate it.

Nora appeared.

The two women looked at one another.

"Good year for raspberries," said Nora.

V said nothing.

"OK, I shoulda kept my big mouth shut," said Nora. "You come all this distance and I just mouth off."

V looked down at the ground. "It's lies, you know, it's really lies and he really is awful. I can't stand it – he's awful."

Nora said again, "I shoulda kept my mouth shut."

The two women picked a few berries. Nora handed hers to V, who accepted them. They went back to the picnic table together, not speaking.

Nora called V after she got back to Oregon. The two women talked about Babs' work with 2nd graders and Caddie's handling of city officials. Nora told V about distant relatives who moved to Idaho and her sons' stepchildren. Neither mentioned politics. Just as she was about to hang up, Nora said to V, "You know, Tiny, I love you."

Later, V thought, "She always says that." V's siblings never said anything about love, even when she knew they thought it. But Nora said it out loud – and V had said it back. "I love you too."

V didn't tell Caddie or Con about the scene at the picnic table. She was ashamed of Nora. She was ashamed of her shame. Nora knew that V thought of her as ignorant, uneducated, someone she had grown away from. And yet Nora called, every Sunday. And reminded her that they were still bonded, that they had taken an oath, that they loved one another. Nora had taken care of Em and Eddie. Nora had stayed at home while V moved further and further away. And now called every week. And told V that she loved her.

Orrville, Pennsylvania, 2018

And then, Babs called.

"Mom is dying."

V flew east the next day. An aggressive brain tumor, hospice, a weak and confused Nora, a spent and apologetic daughter. "Mom didn't want me to call you. But I decided to anyway. Now she's mad, when she remembers, but I think she'll be glad to see you."

They went in through the peeling back door of the house because the steps in front were dangerous.

The hospital bed filled the front room. Only a small path was open to the bedside. Every surface – end tables, chairs, couch -- was piled with papers and knick-knacks and vases with dead flowers.

"Em, what in God's name you doin' here?" Nora's voice scarcely rose above a whisper.

"It's V, Nora. I heard you weren't doing so good."

"I'm fine, but Em, I thought you were at home. Who the hell are you, anyway?"

Babs started to say something, but V held up her hand. Then she took Nora's fingers into her own.

"Hey, lady, how ya doin'? she said softly.

"Not so good, Val. I been better. Had a good day yesterday so s'pose a good one tomorrow. Make yourself some coffee. Instant. Cupboard."

V nodded. "Good idea. I'll do that."

Nora closed her eyes. "Later, I'll take you home. I know you want to go home."

V continued to hold Nora's thin white hand. "That will be good. Maybe we could stop up the mountain – I'm not too old to go down the trail again."

Nora opened her eyes. "I want to go home, you know. They won't let me, but I'm going to go home -- just as soon as I get dressed."

V smiled at Nora. "We'll go home. We'll watch out for the jimson weed. You'll get your shoes all muddy. And we'll lay down on the moss and eat violets."

Nora closed her eyes. V sat in the dark hot room.

V thought of the light-filled house back in Portland. She and Con had kept it open, with lots of space and few furnishings.

Its windows looked out on V's garden, her tangles of foliage and flowers. The oak flooring gleamed in the sunlight; the white walls framed V's paintings of deserts and mountains and big skies.

V thought of the worn-down Pennsylvania mountains and how she had walked up one of them, claiming it as her own place. The West Coast Cascades near Portland were steep-sided and rocky. The trees darkened the trails, and V was always uneasy when she hiked them. She never found any teaberries or trailing pine.

V turned back to Nora and sang softly: "And he walked with me/ And he talked with me/ And he told me I was his own…." Nora closed her eyes and snored lightly.

V got up to boil water for the Nescafe Babs had put on the counter. Babs looked at her, with tears. V smiled.

"You look like my mom," said Babs.

V turned back to the stove, turned on the burner under the kettle, then used her phone to arrange her flight, home.

MAGDALENA GOES TO DUNSMUIR

I

Magdalena pulled off her magenta scarf, flinging it wide as she opened up her arms.

"Willie! Willie, me darling," she called. "I did it. I went to Dunsmuir. You've never seen such an adventure!"

I was sitting in my corner at Monti's Café when Maggie popped in, all gussied up a fire-engine red skirt, orange blouse and purple velvet vest. Unlike Maggie, I'm a blue-jeans type person and I don't go adventuring. Jake loves staying home. With me. And I'm content with that.

Jake and me – we've been married five or so years – mumble along pretty well together. He keeps me out of trouble, and I keep him cheerful. And I have Monti's, where I sit and nod at people who walk by, so that I have my own friends, too. I can eavesdrop on people's stories in Monti's and then tell Jake about them when I get home. He likes that. Otherwise, my life is pretty slow and easy. I had enough trouble to last me when I was young.

So there I was, at Monti's on a Wednesday afternoon, with my book and mimosa, and Maggie – Magdalena, as she prefers

– swishes in with her fancy bracelets and lets us all know -- but me especially -- that she has a new tale to tell.

"I did it. I finally went to Dunsmuir. It was glorious!" Maggie plopped down on the chair across from me, her skirts floating up.

"Dunsmuir? In Scotland?" I vaguely remembered Dunsmuir. Or Denmark? My mind wandered. I hadn't thought about Dunsmuir and Hamlet since 10th grade.

"Nah, not in Scotland," said Ralph. Ralph was sitting at my table – the café was crowded – without being invited of course. Of course Ralph knew that Dunsmuir was not in Scotland. Ralph knows everything. "Dunsmuir is in Canada – Vancouver Island," he said.

Ralph and I had nodded at one another when he sat down, and then we took up our books, mine about silk cloth and his on the Roman Empire. We don't talk much as a rule.

"No, no, no, not Canada, dummy." Magdalena smirked at him. "You don't even know what's down the road. Dunsmuir, California. Northern California. First stop south after Oregon on the Amtrak." Magdalena smiled sweetly.

"Amtrak?" I said. "You traveled by Amtrak?"

Few people I know take the Amtrak from Portland to California – it takes days to get anywhere – and for sure no one gets off north of Oakland. I once took the train south, on a lark, with a beau of mine. But we didn't get off at Dunsmuir.

"It was great," said Maggie. "You meet the most interesting people – the young guy I was sitting with told me his pants were too tight and I suggested he buy a larger size. He said I reminded him of his grandmother, and he fell asleep on my shoulder. His hair grease was a mess, and I finally put a bunch of Kleenex between his head and my shoulder and that woke him up and he got grouchy, so I moved into an empty seat across the aisle. It'll take some doing to get that grease out of his seatback, I'm telling you."

"You went by coach? Not a sleeper? To Dunsmuir?" I was still trying to get hold of her story.

"And then, in Klamath Falls, an old lady got into the train and sat down beside me and she had a cat curled up under her coat. I don't think cats are allowed on Amtrak. We got to talking and she told me about how she had a collapsible cat box that she stuck into her purse and when 'kitty tells me she has to go, I just go to the rest room and take care of her needs.' Well, it takes all kinds, I'm telling you, and kitty spent most of her time fast asleep. Turns out the old lady was going to Dunsmuir too."

"Dunsmuir – for God's sake – how long did it take?" Ralph was aggrieved. "Why didn't you fly or something? And why Dunsmuir? I mean, who's in Dunsmuir? What's in Dunsmuir? Where is it, anyway?"

I was remembering a road atlas that Jake and I used on a trip to California once. "Ashland's the last town in southern Oregon and after that – well, there's Mt Shasta in California and I remember Weed on I-5, but Weed – well, it has a gas station and a diner-ish sort of place, but…."

"Willie, my dear," said Magdalena, beaming at me, "Weed is north of Dunsmuir, although Amtrak doesn't go to Weed. It doesn't go to Ashland either. It takes off east at Eugene, goes over the mountains to Klamath Falls – that's where the cat lady got on – and then comes back through the mountains and rumbles on to Dunsmuir.

"I'm sorry, but why did you go to Dunsmuir? I mean...." I was still sort of confused.

Ralph put his book aside.

"Because it's there," said Maggie. "Dunsmuir isn't near anything but Mt Shasta. And sorta near Weed. It's a long way to Sacramento, and even further to Oakland, where you can get a bus into San Francisco, which I've been to. But I'd never been to Dunsmuir so...."

"I've never been to Bangladesh, either, but I don't think I'd take the train – by coach – to get there. But of course," Ralph said, sarcastically. "I always wanted to go to Dunsmuir.

"How big is Dunsmuir?" Ralph liked facts.

"Oh, it spreads out a long way along the tracks," said Maggie, "and you can get into the mountains from there, mostly on hiking trails and such. There's lots of waterfalls. And a sorta – um – gourmet restaurant." Magdalena's explanation did not explain much.

Ralph turned on his patient voice. "How many people live in Dunsmuir? And why does the train stop there?"

"Oh, I dunno," she replied. "Maybe a couple thousand. There's a Super 8 motel and resort thingies that have box cars for lodging. And a little downtown just up the hill– that's where I stayed. In an old hotel, all tarted up with calicos and doilies and long velvet curtains. It has wide wooden stairs with carved handrails. And the cat lady's brother, who manages the train station, told me to be careful – actually he's her brother-in-law and doesn't manage the station but was there to pick up her up...."

"Wait." I was remembering the Amtrak trip and Dunsmuir. "The train stops in Dunsmuir for about 20 seconds, right? It stops in the middle of the night. I mean the deep dark middle of the night. And there's a station? That's open? Well, that's useful for old ladies who are getting off the train at 2 a.m. and don't have a brother-in-law to meet them. Was there a taxi?"

"No, no, Willie," Magdelena used her patient voice (she often did so when I fussed at her about the kinds of things she got up to, at her age.)

"It wasn't the middle of the night. The train was on time, so it was only 12:45 a.m. – or thereabouts – and no, there's no taxi. The hotel is just a couple of blocks from the station, and I was going to walk, only it turned out it's straight uphill and I did have a big suitcase or two and my carry-on and the brother-in-law of the cat lady offered me a ride – he said I shouldn't be out on the streets alone, but for god's sake, I'm 75 years old."

I noted, silently, that she had subtracted a year or two from her age.

"And no one was going to molest me," Magdalena continued. "Especially not on a dark night in the middle of the mountains. But anyway, the wind was blowing sideways and it was raining, so I accepted the ride, and after settling the cat's business, we all got into the big-wheeled pick-up and drove up the hill.

"I got into the hotel all right – the brother-in-law waited to make sure – nobody at the desk, but they had those punch-in-number thingies, so I waved the truck on. A note on the desk said if no clerk was available, just to sign the register and use my punch-in numbers for my room.

"I had forgotten about stairs, though, which was a problem. I had reserved room 301 because they called it 'An Attic Rendezvous' and said it had a great view." She frowned.

"I couldn't lug those suitcases up the stairs, even though I only had three with me. So I sat down in the lobby for a minute and may have fallen asleep but when I woke up I decided I could get up to my room if I left my bags behind the desk. So I stuffed some toiletries into my purse, grabbed night clothes from a suitcase, and went up the stairs. It was a long way to the second floor. And then, another flight in front of me. Someone opened a door behind me, but I didn't look back –I didn't want to meet a stranger in the middle of the night."

I was gobsmacked. "You got into town at 12:45 a.m., caught a ride in a strange pick-up truck, let yourself into a deserted hotel on a deserted street, left your luggage in the lobby and climbed two flights of stairs, looking over your shoulder for the ax murderer?"

"But you're still alive. And unscarred. No ax murderer, then?" Ralph rolled his eyes.

"Oh no," Magdalena put on her sweet voice again. "Everyone was just as nice as nice could be. And the next morning, when I told the desk gal that the water wasn't coming out of the faucets in my bathroom, they transferred me to their street level suite, which was very lovely and even had a private patio.

"And I met the loveliest man, just a sweetheart. Tall, dark, and handsome, as they say. And almost our age. It was perfectly divine.

"But, here's Bridget Clare with my mimosa, and I'm meeting the gals for late lunch, so bye-bye." She swirled around and headed for the back of Monti's.

To Ralph she said, "Enjoy watching Rome fall."

And off she went, with a jingle and a swish, to the end table, full of women, from which air kisses flew and exclamations of pleasure could be heard.

Ralph and I looked at each other and then went back to our books. I found myself thinking about Maggie, all alone, meeting strange men in a deserted town, on a lark on the Amtrak. Must have turned out OK 'cause here she was.

II

A few weeks later, I found Magdalena in the nearly deserted café, near my table. She was alone and sitting real quiet. I sat down across from her.

"Hey lady, what's up?" I said.

Magdalena sat up and smiled brightly. "Hey, hi Willie. I'm just sitting here thinking."

"Um," I said. "Well, thinkin' – thinkin's dangerous -- can getcha into lots of trouble."

"Well, sometimes a person has to take time off to think, right?" she said. "But you know, the other day, I never did finish my tale of Dunsmuir. I could see Ralph was just dying to get back to his Caligulas."

"There's more?" I didn't know what she was talking about with Ralph, but her tale of Dunsmuir certainly had more to it. Of course there was more.

"No water in my attic room. That was the first thing. And two flights of stairs which I had to climb down in my nightgown – I'd call it a negligee but that would be a tad much – to get a clean set of clothes for breakfast.

"And then, in the lobby, sitting with a cup of coffee and a paper, was the loveliest looking fellow. He had streaks of silver in his perfectly groomed hair – I should ask about his hairdresser. Kissable lips and a good smile – lots of teeth. And me, without my teeth even brushed. Luckily I had a nice silk robe – the blue one – over my old cotton nightie, so I was decent. Anyway, there was someone at the desk, and I told her my troubles – and the fellow with the eyelashes and white teeth was listening, I could tell – and she, the clerk, I mean, such a darling, she offered to exchange my mountaintop room for the first floor suite, which was really nice, with its own living room and patio and kitchenette as well as a great bathroom – big, with hot water and good make-up lights. I agreed that that sounded like a fair trade for not being able to wash my face, and we were all set."

"Well, that's looking up," I said. "At least if the ax murderer is going to get you, he won't have to climb the stairs." I gulped my mimosa, thinking this might be a two-drink day.

"The thing is, things went on pretty good from there and I stayed in Dunsmuir for three days and had a fine time and then came home and, well, the gentleman with the coffee bought me breakfast in Dunsmuir after I got respectable and we got acquainted and that was great and then I came home and…."

"You came back on the Amtrak?" I asked.

"Oh no," said Maggie. "He was going to Seattle – his name is Reginald – Reggie – and he had to go right by Portland, so he drove me home from Dunsmuir in his Jaguar – right up to my door and helped me in with my bags and is coming back this weekend. Nice car – and he drives well. He has the most gorgeous long fingers."

Ah, I thought. A development. A Man. Magdalena had lost her husband to a heart attack a few years earlier. She looked young for an 80-year-old but I never heard her talk about any men friends before.

"So," I was a bit hesitant to say it. "He's coming back down from Seattle this weekend – to stay – with you?"

"Well, of course." Maggie smiled a big smile. "We got to be friends, see, and he's a widower and at loose ends and one thing led to another – those north woods waterfalls are really romantic – anyway, he's coming down again this weekend. I'm trying to work out what to wear."

"How old is this guy, anyway?" My voice had started to get an edge, but Magdalena, perhaps thinking about Dunsmuir and the waterfalls, didn't notice.

"Oh, late 60s, maybe early 70s. He's really well put together and has such a sweet manner. He brought me roses one evening – I'm not sure where he got them, but he's good at things like that. And he cajoled the desk clerk into getting her mother to cook us a full course meal because the restaurants in Dunsmuir are, well, you know....

"The desk clerk's mother? You gotta be kidding. No desk clerk ever has a mother." I got distracted, wondering if I could remember any motel desk clerks from my travels. "Was she the one who wasn't there the night you showed up with three suitcases and a carry-on?"

"No, no," said Maggie. "She was great. Dunsmuir is a tiny town, really. The mother had been a professional chef and retired to Dunsmuir because the daughter wanted to hike the Pacific Coast Trail in bits and pieces, which she does, and when she's broke, she works at the hotel. And she – the daughter,

I mean – was really interested in Reginald – Reggie – he's so good with people and had chatted her up. No one else was at the hotel, so when he started escorting me, he figured I deserved a good meal on my last evening in Dunsmuir, so he flirted with the lovely young thing until she told him about her mother and offered to set him up with a good meal. The hotel has a nice private area with a table and she brought candles and Reggie produced a bottle of champagne and, I mean, it was wonderful. Her mother really can cook. And then he asked me if I would like a ride in his Jaguar back to Portland, and of course I said yes."

"And so he dropped you off and will return this weekend?"

"Well, that was a couple of weeks ago. He stayed over for a bit – he's retired and has a condo near the Seattle waterfront, and he didn't need to be back for anything, so I gave him a tour of Laurelhurst and Alameda Ridge and the Japanese Gardens. We had a lovely time. Went to the opera – I have season tickets – and to the art museum and he got his Jaguar serviced while he was here. I had to pay for that because his credit card was on the fritz, but that wasn't a problem – no one blinks an eye when an old lady pays for things these days."

"So why are you sitting here sulking?" I asked.

"I'm not sulking," Maggie sniffed at me a little. "I'm thinking."

"About what?"

We both sipped on our drinks. I thought about getting another one.

"Oh," she said brightly, "Dunsmuir and the waterfalls and the spa bathtub."

Her voice dropped. "You know, it's a podunk little town. The storefronts are boarded up and the best waterfall is illegal to visit because it's right up the hill from the train tracks, and some idiot tourist got hit by a train a while back, so there are all these signs 'No trespassing; danger, danger, danger' and the waterfall really is beautiful."

"Wait – you went past the no trespassing signs, across the tracks, to see a waterfall? There aren't enough of them in the Columbia Gorge?"

"It wasn't all that dangerous," Maggie objected." Just steep slopes on either side of the tracks and then the canyon and the water itself. The falls are named Mossbrae, for the hotel, and it's gorgeous and just about the only walkable sight in town, although we did go to the city park up the street where there's a pedestrian bridge across the tracks and that was kind of nice, although windy. It was windy the whole time I was there, so we didn't go out much, but my room, my room was a delight."

"Oh Magdalena…." I was seeing the larger picture. My stomach rolled over. Men can't be trusted when they are young, and when they get old and women get older, they can be bad. Really, really bad. Although my Jake is an exception, but even so, you don't find many exceptions out there.

"Well, see," she said, making a little face. "How often do you get to spend time with a buff guy, playing poker and whatnot, a guy who can sweet talk a hotel clerk into a dinner for two by candle light and who drives a Jaguar and offers you a ride of 200 miles, just because he likes your company?"

"He seemed to have liked your company," I said, hoping I didn't sound like Ralph. "What did you do in Portland?"

"Oh, I already told you – the usual – opera, gardens, walks around the neighborhood. One day he rented bikes and we rode a little – I put on my best Spanx pants, the ones I don't get to wear much anymore. And of course, I got dressed up for the opera and he had his Jaguar and the valet was really impressed and happy to park it and so charming that I had to tip him extra – Reginald isn't a great tipper – but anyway, he likes doing just what I like. We went to a Chamber Music Northwest concert, and he took me to that new hotel on Fifth, The Savoy, for drinks. The view from the bar is stunning. He said some time when we were feeling jaded, we would stay there for a weekend. He's just that kind of guy, you know." Maggie smiled a bit smugly.

"And so -- why are you … thinking?" I asked. All this prancing around Portland, she in her shiny, gorgeous clothes, and roaring about in his Jaguar. It didn't seem quite right for an old woman. I wouldn't have been taken in, and I was anxious about Magdalena's being played for a fool. I thought she was smarter than that.

"I was hoping Ralph would come in. I wanted to ask him about something" she said.

"Ralph! Why Ralph? Do you really need a history lesson? On Dunsmuir?"

"Just a minute. I need another mimosa. Can I get you one?" And without waiting for my nod and taking my glass, off she went, all tinkles and jingles and swirling skirts. And then she was back with an orange-cranberry and a pink mimosa.

"Pomegranate," she said, pointing at her pink choice. "Monti's finally got a new flavor. About time. The drinks we had at The Savoy were stupendous – they cost $25 bucks apiece, which is a bit steep, but well worth it."

Mimosas at Monti's are $6.50 and have been that price for at least five years. Before that, they were $6.00, and when the price went up you could hear the howls for blocks around. I myself did not complain, only wondered why fifty cents and not a nice round dollar.

Magdalena continued her story. "I had to up the tip that Reginald left, and I told him about it after we got back to the house. He pretended to be surprised, but I knew it was one of his habits, like not having a working credit card. I didn't mind paying, you understand, it's just one of his habits, a hole in his ethical standards. But where's Ralph today?"

"Haven't seen him," I answered. "Why do you want to see Ralph?"

"Well, Willie," she slowed her speech. "I'm thinking that he -- Ralph, I mean -- knows something, I mean things, about finances and things, and I just wanted to ask him a question." She was moving her mimosa around the tabletop.

"Finances?" I asked.

"I dunno, Willie. Protecting one's money, investing – things like that."

"So your new boyfriend is setting you up, eh?" I said. "Prenups starting to raise their ugly heads." I forgot to be tactful. She paid no attention.

"Reginald says that in three weeks he's coming down for a meeting, and we're going to The Savoy for the weekend as well as drinks, and he wants me to dress up. Which I will do because I love dressing up. But – I got to thinking about his tone and everything. So now, well, I just thought I'd check in with Ralph a bit."

"Oh Maggie."

And then the café filled up and a number of her friends came by to check in. I had to get home – Jake was waiting to take me to the dentist. The subject of her toy-boy was set aside.

III

Ralph was by himself at a table next time I went to Monti's. It had been a while. I had had a tooth taken out and had been avoiding mimosas until I got off the pain pills. I started past Ralph's table, but he cocked his head at me and gestured at a chair. I sat down.

"Hey, Willie, did Magdalena talk to you about her boyfriend?" he asked.

"You mean Reginald? Well, yes, a little." I was wary. Ralph was gonna pry Maggie's secrets out of me.

"He's a con job. You know that, right?" Ralph sounded quite cheerful.

"I did wonder. But she sounded so happy...."

Although as soon as I said it, I knew Magdalena was worried. I'm too cautious and too mousy to be interesting to con men. No one would mistake me for an available widow. But Magdalena seemed frivolous and – although I'd never dare say it out loud – a little foolish.

"She said something about wanting to see you." I said to Ralph. "What for?"

"Well," suddenly Ralph sounded cagey. "I can't tell tales out of school and she was vague, but apparently, this Reginald guy – Reggie! --has designs on her. They have plans for a big evening, a special evening, she's to get all dressed up and they'll go to The Savoy, and it turns out she isn't as spacey as I thought she was. I mean, an old lady, over the moon about this young guy, you know."

"Um, how not spacey?" Magdalena was often a sucker for other people. She was always loaning her silk skirts to her friends, and she lost money when they played bridge. She was friends with every Tom, Dick, and Harry in Monti's, including Ralph, which tells you something.

"Well, I can't tell tales out of office…," he said, and proceeded to tell the tale. "Maggie wanted financial and legal advice, like how to tie her money up so only she could get at it, stuff like that. And I'm not an accountant or lawyer. So I told her what I thought, and I sent her downtown to Biggers, Bags, and Louie. They handle my money. I told her I would call them and say she was coming, but when I offered to pay, she got insulted. It'll cost her a pretty penny. I told her that, but she waved me off. So I put in the phone call – the head guy there is an old friend – and I was wondering – have you seen her lately?"

I went silent. I didn't like the looks of Reggie in spite of his Jaguar, and Magdalena, while well off, didn't act like she was rich. And she was definitely old. It was all a bit much, too much like an old tiresome bum's trick. I needed to think about it.

I said as much to Ralph and he shrugged and went back to his book. I moved to another table and got a refill on my coffee.

IV

The next day at Monti's, I sat with Magdalena.

"What are you up to?" I asked.

"What do you mean, Willie? I'm just sitting here in Monti's, on a cold Wednesday afternoon, enjoying my mimosa." She opened her mascaraed eyes wide, smiled at me, and then glanced around the room, vacantly.

"I talked to Ralph yesterday. You aren't falling for that Reginald guy, are you? The one who makes you pay for tips and repairs to his jalopy and who knows what else. I mean, it's the oldest con game in the world. Even if he's handsome and fun, you can't afford an expensive male child when you're approaching 80."

Magdalena looked at me. Then she sighed and put her mimosa down on the table.

"OK. OK. I know. I know. He's a grifter. A good-looking one. Probably gambles. Certainly runs with an iffy crowd in Seattle. But he's also sweet and lots of fun. Dunsmuir exceeded all my expectations – not that they were very high – and he did give me that ride. And he does wash bare backs very nicely. Which is important."

This memory cheered her up. Also she was hoping to shock me and make me forget to give her the stink eye.

"So," I said, "if you know he's out for your money, why are you still seeing him? Staying at The Savoy will cost you a couple thou, just for the bed, which you could have for free at home. And don't tell me he's paying. He'll have lost his wallet or forgotten his credit card – or worse, he'll pay with a loan from a shady buddy that he'll promise to pay back after he marries you!"

I saw it all. The Savoy. The champagne on ice. A photographer. The proposal, Reggie-boy on his knees. The big suite with orchids and the insistence on getting married, as soon as possible. I never thought Magdalena was one to fall for that kind of scheme.

I have read all about how elderly widows get taken. I married my Jake because he was down-to-earth and a gentleman who always paid when we went out to dinner. And we have separate bank accounts. We split house bills, and he even pays for his spendy screwdrivers. I pay for my coffee at Monti's, and we live in a tiny house by the freeway. My money is going to my daughters.

I mean, you have to be careful. Even when you are young, you have to watch out. Being shoved around and having to hand over the rent money to pay for booze can get old real fast.

Maggie pulled me back.

"So Ralph's been talking, eh? Geez, Willie, you are sorta slow." Magdalena grinned. "I saw all that when he gave me the agenda for the weekend. I'm prepared."

And with that, she got up, took a seat next to Ralph, where he sat next to the door. I was dismissed.

V

"So what do you think of Mag's scheme?" Ralph came to sit down with me after Magdalena left.

I didn't want him to know she hadn't actually told me of any scheme except to be robbed and left heartbroken and moneyless. "Um," I said. "Do you think she can get away with it?"

Ralph lowered his voice. "She's a pip. A real pip. She's annoyed with Reggie-baby for sticking her with the Jaguar repair bill. She paid because she's good-hearted and did get that ride home, but she's onto him." Ralph smiled a big smile.

"What does he think he was going to get out of her, anyway? I asked. "She really isn't a Jaguar owner – Amtrak by coach, for heaven's sake – and while the Laurelhurst house is pretty fancy, it was her husband's. She doesn't have enough money to go all-out Savoy, does she?"

"Dear Willie. You are naïve. If her husband had a Laurelhurst house, and she still maintains it, there's money there. Between you and me, there's a lot of money there." Ralph almost winked at me. "Just because she hangs out for the mimosas here at Monti's doesn't mean that she isn't well off. Our Maggie is not only nobody's fool, she's also been taking care of her own money for some years. And she knows about the ways of pretty men."

And with that pronouncement, Ralph went back to his book.

I waited for more, but he refused to look up. I pulled on my coat and walked home, slowly. All this was new to me, conmen and rich friends. Not at Monti's. Not my style. Monti's wasn't for rich widows – or at least I didn't think so. And all this folderol because she took the train, not even a sleeper, to northern California, home of Bigfoot and ex-loggers and marijuana. I had to think about this. The thought of that hustler – Reggie! -- shook me up, although thinking about Jake, at home watching baseball, helped me breathe a little better.

VI

A week or so later, I found Magdalena sitting by herself at one of Monti's big tables. I helped myself to a seat where we could both see the rest of the café.

"So. How are you, anyway? And what's up?" I had to ask.

"Hello, Willie, m'dear, how are you today? I am fine!" Maggie's voice spread out in that too-loud way.

"Talked to Ralph?" I asked?

"Ah, yes. Ralph. He was very helpful. And I got some other help, too. I couldn't approach old Ernst Adams, my family lawyer – he would have made a big fuss. But Ralph's guys handled it all without an ounce of dither. So, I'm good."

"OK, Magdalena." I could not stand not knowing one more minute. "Spill the beans. What happened at The Savoy? And to your boyfriend? And what's with the lawyers?"

Magdalena sighed. "We need a mimosa."

"Get me a coffee," I called. And off she swirled and brought back two rim-full glasses.

"You see," she said, after a quick sip, "I wondered about him when he took advantage of the nice desk clerk in Dunsmuir and stuck me with the repair bill. Actually, by that time, I had figured him for a con-man. But he was delicious to have around. And I could afford him at that level."

"You didn't mind paying to repair a Jaguar?" My eyes got a bit wider.

"Well, when Arthur died, he left me a lot of money, more than I deserve. And I've given some of it away, but mostly it just sits there, making more faster than I can spend it. And so this year I decided I was going to change.

"Arthur liked fancy things, cruises and first class plane tickets to Hawaii. He always wanted to treat me to the most expensive things, and I gave into him, even when I wanted to come to Monti's with the ragamuffins."

She didn't notice my wince.

"I wanted to try out some different ways to have fun, like he and I used to before he decided that spending money was the point of it all. Arthur is dead, and I'm still alive!"

"The trip to Dunsmuir was impulsive," she continued. "I had never traveled by coach on the train, so I looked at the Amtrak map and found a totally unheard-of place to check out. And Reginald -- well – I never had a boy-toy before, so, why not? But the big doe eyes and courtship and invitation to a weekend at The Savoy brought things to a head. So the banker-lawyers organized things for me, very nicely, even if they were expensive."

"So you didn't go for the weekend with Reginald?"

"Oh no, I went. I had promised, and it sounded like fun. It was fun. Reggie's really quite good at being charming. And he asked me to marry him and I went along with it, although I told him I needed the weekend to think about it. So we had a merry old time – spa back rubs and gorgeous flowers in the suite – and then on Sunday, over breakfast, I told him I had been thinking about it and I pulled out the papers that the lawyers had prepared and said that before I committed, I needed him to sign some things.

"That was fun, too. When I told the lawyers what I had in mind, they looked solemn, and said it was gonna be expensive– billable hours, you know– and necessitating, as it would, that it be iron-clad. I suggested that the wording be strong– separate bank accounts and credit cards, no sharing of monies while I was alive and nothing whatsoever at my death.

"Also I wanted Reggie to know with precision what was expected – clarity about sharing marriage chores, like vacuuming and cooking and laundry, so he would be put on notice that I don't have a butler and maids. And, as a final statement, in the future he was to be responsible for the repairs to any personal property he owned, like clothing – and cars."

"In other words, a legalized squeeze." I couldn't quite restrain my giggle. Magdalena beamed.

"Oh, geez, Willie, giving him that stack of bespoke stationery, with all its 'Whereas'es' and 'Party of the First,' was just delish. During the weekend he worked the adoring suitor bit, but I got tired of his moony eyes. And when I handed him the papers and he started going through them, he got red in the face and I noticed his nose was redder than his cheeks, and he started growling at me, in a kind of low, ugly voice. So I stuck my nose up in the air, got up out of my seat, and went and checked out – the Savoy will pack your bags for you and send them along – the concierge got me a taxi before I finished at the desk, and off I sailed.

"I always wanted to sail away from a smarmy con-man and – well, a bit like going to Dunsmuir – it was mighty satisfying.

"And when I got home I texted Ralph and invited him to dinner at Pastini's, as a thank you."

I sat back and looked at her.

"And we had dinner at Pastini's – you know that Italian chain – we went to the one on Broadway, where that waitress, Billie, works. She always tells raunchy stories about internet dating, and she has a 20-some-year-old daughter who keeps her out of trouble – when Arthur was alive I sometimes snuck out to Pastini's. I like the meatballs and I wanted Ralph to meet Billie.

"And Ralph paid. In cash. And let me tip if I promised to have dinner with him next week. And so of course I will. Unless I go to Tukwila. On the Amtrak, of course.

"But there's Karen at her table, and she wants me to join her knitting group, so I will join, but only if it includes wine-tasting. Ta-ta." And off she went.

I sat for a minute, and then walked home, very slowly. When I had taken off my coat in the house, I sat down on the couch beside Jake. He muted his baseball game and asked me how it was going.

"I'm gonna make reservations to take the Amtrak to Dunsmuir," I said. "There's an old hotel that they've fixed up, all fancy. I wanna to see it. And the famous waterfall."

He looked startled. "Well, that's great," he said after a while. "We can go after the football playoffs –TV in Dunsmuir might not be good. I guess I can miss a basketball game or two."

I looked at him and smiled.

"I'm going by myself," I said. "Maybe by coach – I'll have to think about it. And you won't have to miss any games."

I reached over and patted his arm. "I think I need to get out of town a little," I said. "But I might have to buy some new clothes."

Jake stared at me, smiled and nodded, and then turned the TV sound back on.

I went to my computer to look up Dunsmuir and the Amtrak schedule.

ON THE RIVER

I

The two men stood at the edge of the one-lane concrete bridge, stripping off their shirts, then unbuckling and dropping their pants. Underneath the clothes their skin glimmered in the bright sunlight, interrupted by black swim trunks. Black hair on the head of one made a rhythm of vertical contrasts. Its mass blurred in the slight breeze off the water. The other male's hair was a pool of shiny yellow around indistinct features.

V watched them from the far side of the small bridge. The sky, bleached murky white by the sun, arched over the sparse landscape. Eastern Oregon's black-shadowed pines and buff-colored undergrowth, high on the ridge above the water, radiated heat. The river, contrasting with the bowl of sky and land, carved a narrow canyon into the steep-sided ravine.

V felt her body relax into its loose black pants and sneakers. She felt part of the scene – warm and a bit dusty. It was good to let her early fog dissipate. Her vision, always worse in the morning, had seemed particularly incoherent. The smudged outlines and lack of details irritated her. As a painter, V had always maintained that detail was the essential ingredient for a good painting. Now, it was detail that eluded her.

But this morning, she found herself relaxing into the sun's warmth and the contrasts of light and shade. She had always found young bodies with their carved muscles and taut skin wonderful to observe. What she saw now was light, gleaming, bouncing off everything, stopped by black accents. The river, along which she and Conrad had just hiked, had been wide and shallow, a golden-brown. But here the stream got shoved together by the rising ground and had become a funnel, fierce with its near black currents.

V eyed two young women, clad in bright shorts and tops, standing nearby. They were also watching the men. One of them turned to her, saying "We didn't bring suits – it's really a guy thing."

The other, lips full in red lipstick, nodded, and they all turned back to the men.

The blond male bent over the side of the bridge, and then turned his head and shook it. His hair flickered in the sunlight.

The dark-haired one coached his friend, yelling against the river's roar: "You have to go into the funnel, the deepest water, about 15 feet deep. I go feet first…" The big guy demonstrated how he moved his arms and shoulders, lengthening them out, and bringing them down to his sides. Light flashed as he gestured.

"No cannon ball?" the younger man yelled back.

"No, no, legs straight down – don't worry – the current will catch you before you hit bottom. Some people use stiff arms and shoulders but I keep loose. Go with the current and use your arms to steer toward the shore. It's shallow downstream -- you won't drown --but walking back to the bridge is hard on the feet. So head to the shore as soon as you can." The black-haired guy was loud and cheerful.

V noted, not for the first time, that her hearing was sharp and easy, but she had to squint to make out edges. She heard herself sigh. She saw Con glance at her. He said nothing.

"How many times have you done this?" the blond called.

"Oh, ten, fifteen or so," yelled the other. "It's really cold – you lose your breath – but you'll love it. Just go in, feet first, arms loose, and head to the right as you come up."

And then off he leapt, into the water, splash covered by the water's roar. His friend took a deep breath and, flashing a head turn at the young women, followed.

A great yell echoed under the bridge and on the other side came black hair and white skin. V watched as the river angled over the fuzzy outlines of the man's body. The swimmer pushed toward the gray boulder next to the path along the water's edge. And then came the other white body, working hard, more smudged, reaching up a hand for help from his friend as he flailed his way through the water.

"Amazing!" yelled the black-haired one. The blond struggled out of the water and shook himself.

"Again!" shouted the dark-haired leader.

The girls shook their heads, hair swinging from their faces. They appeared athletic, dressed in shorts and trainers, and V could see the curve of muscle in their arms. They would probably do OK in the stream, but they made no move toward the far edge of the bridge.

The two men came back up the path to the bridge and repeated their jumps, black-first, then blond. Again they were smudged by the waves and reflections and black water. They were sleek, well-furred fuzzes, like white seals with black markings.

"If I were thirty-five," said V to Conrad, "I'd strip to my underwear and jump in."

She had put on black underwear that morning, and for a second, she imagined how she might look.

"Oh God, V" said Conrad. "You couldn't pay me."

He laughed and then drew himself up a bit. His skinny torso, bent by his arthritic spine, curved over the edge of the bridge. He continued looking for fish along the inlet beyond the path.

"And I couldn't haul you out, either," he added, without looking at her. "You'd have to drag yourself up by your crooked pinkies."

V pretended to shove him and smiled. The old couple had long ago perfected their personas, she, exuberant, and impulsive, and he, funny with the voice of ironic wisdom. It was a performance, but one grounded in mutual appreciation.

The blond, standing on the path next to the stream, glanced up at the two old ones watching from above.

"It was great!" he yelled to them with a big smile. "You should try it!"

One of the girls handed him a towel and he kissed her lightly on the cheek. Then they walked together to the car where the men changed into dry clothes. V watched the vague shapes in silence.

Their skin had been warmly white, she noted. Pacific Northwest skin seldom achieves a deep California tan. But in the summer sun and against the black bathing suits, the men's flesh had shone, velvety and magnificent.

II

V and Conrad were staying at a vacation cabin two miles upriver. They had come to eastern Oregon from Portland after a summer filled with medical appointments, surgical procedures, and the deaths of four elderly friends. The deaths – four in three months -- were obscene, V thought -- and involved much phoning and consolation notes and personal histories to rummage through. V's eye procedures hadn't improved her vision much, and the writing and reading of bad news didn't help. The summer weather at their home on the western side of the Cascades had been beautiful but, as even stay-at-home Conrad admitted, "not all that much fun."

Their stroll to the bridge had been unintentionally long. They thought the trail map showed it to be about a mile. When the river path stretched beyond that, the enticement of the burbling water, the occasional wildflower, and the warm sun encouraged them to keep walking. But now they had to make the return trip. They started back up the path along the riverside.

V adjusted her sunglasses and pulled her hat down her forehead. Her replacement knee began its streak of pain, and the light reflecting upward from the river hurt her eyes. She limped but moved doggedly.

"Oh my God!"

Conrad's voice was quiet but hard and intent. He had stopped and was looking across the river at a sparsely forested hillside, awash with dune-colored grasses, spiked with ponderosa and fir.

"It's an eagle! A golden eagle!"

V narrowed her eyes and looked. She saw the ponderosas' shapes against the light grasses.

"It's up ahead of you, fourth tree from that big fir, almost at the top." Conrad pointed, moving his arm slowly, as birders are taught to do.

V tried to follow his pointing, counting the trees she could see from where she stopped. Conrad was not an official birder, but he loved watching and identifying wildlife. He had read A Salad Only the Devil Would Eat and saw amazing shapes among the urban shrubs and street trees in Portland. V always dutifully looked where he pointed but could seldom see what Conrad saw.

"Holy shit." Con's language disintegrated but stayed quiet. "Oh look, here it comes, down the river."

And then V saw it, outspread wings blotting the desert sky. Glints of gold where a tiny head and beak preceded the huge form, its black wings, feathers spread like fingers, looming as it crossed the river, close enough to make her flinch. Then it soared back across the river, up the steep ravine, and spiked downward, claws outstretched.

"It got it, it caught something – a rabbit, I think, did you see it, V? Did you see it?" Con could scarcely control his voice.

"I saw it." V watched as the bird rose and flew, wriggling mass in its claws, up the side of the hill. "I saw it. I thought it was coming after my hair." V put her hand on the top of her head, as if to protect her wild, silver hair. She felt Con's exultation as well as her own stomach, dropping with fear and awe.

The bird flapped its way into the evergreens and disappeared from view.

"I never thought I'd see a golden eagle," said Conrad, as they continued slowly back along the rutted path.

V concentrated on placing her feet carefully. She was shaking.

"Never," repeated Con. "I've seen bald eagles, but goldens don't like cities; they don't much like people, either. A golden eagle, right there, closer than God." He went silent and turned back to the trail.

V felt again the power of the bird and its glints of light and depths of darkness, its speed and unfathomable dive. She forgot to notice the uncertain footing. They continued up the path toward the coziness of their cabin.

III

Later, plumped down on the deck chairs beside the river, V felt herself aggrieved. She couldn't figure out what was biting at her, so she stared at the water. It wouldn't stand still. It kept moving on. She couldn't quite get a fix on it. It wouldn't settle; it was unstoppable and unseeable. Everything on or in it flowed, just out of focus.

You may never see the same river twice, V thought, but that is not exactly consoling.

It felt good not to be smiling. She stuck her tongue out at the water and made a snarky face. Then she settled more comfortably into her chair, wondering if Conrad had seen her making faces.

Then, across the river, in a smooth dark backwater, she saw a fuzzed ripple that angled from near the shore, making a widening wake as it came toward the water's faster moving center where it disappeared. She looked back at the sheltered edge of the cove where another of the wakes came toward her. Then three appeared from the calm waters further upstream. They all disappeared into the river's swiftly moving center.

V squinted. The backwater was smooth and deep brown-black. The river's center was shallow, full of blue and white ripples above the light tans of the underlying rocks. V could see nothing there except rushing water fizzing out the river bottom. The deep blue of the undersides of the riffles started her wondering what, exactly, to call that color -- blue/black -- reflecting something of the bottom and something of the sky.

She closed her eyes and thought about blues: cobalt, phthalo, cerulean, ultramarine, indigo – oil paint colors.

Maybe watercolor would be better as a painting material, but the range of blues in oils was more expansive. Possibly an abstract, impressionistic, all mist and indefinite line. Yes, watercolor and some kind of misting overlay, the blues overlain with speckled reflections of the gold and red of the larches along the shore.

Conrad had also been watching the wakes in the backwater.

"Hey V, I'm seeing some kind of critter, moving through that inlet across from us. Can't quite tell what it is – a nose or a fin. Some kind of fish I think, although I guess it could be a river otter."

Conrad's description was, as usual, as precise as he could make it.

V looked again but could see nothing but a notch in the smooth water that rippled into a widening wake.

Then Conrad mentioned food and they decided on tuna fish for dinner and the next time V looked, the sun had moved and the river was all-over brown and gray. The wakes had disappeared.

After dinner, they lingered at the deck's picnic table. A stellar jay landed on the railing, brilliant indigo with a black crest. It squawked raucously, but ignored the humans. The black crest that made these jays so easily identified was interrupted by a strip of blue, the same brilliant blue as gleamed down its long tail. Not indigo, V decided. Cerulean with a touch of ultramarine. A chipmunk, almost a brown oxide in color with tan stripes, appeared under the snowberry bushes lining the river bank. It ran under the deck and then back out into the open and up the deck steps. V watched it casually. It wouldn't hold still long enough for her to get a fix on the darker color – perhaps a burnt umber. And the undercolor of the jay escaped her also; it fuzzed into the grays of the deck railing and foliage bark.

A few summers back, a ground squirrel had gotten into V's painting bag and bit open a tube of phthalo blue oil paint. V could still summon up her outrage about that and she wanted to thumb her nose at the chipmunk. Instead, she turned back to her book. Conrad munched on a potato chip.

Suddenly Conrad yelped and stood up, shaking his left leg. The chipmunk dashed away, under V's outstretched foot.

"He got up on my chest. I didn't see him coming until up my leg and onto my chest. Then he ran back down to my thigh! Oh my god, that monkey almost got into my beard."

They both burst out laughing. Conrad brushed himself off, deleting the memory of the tiny claws. He put a potato chip down near the deck steps, and the two of them went back to reading. The evening darkened, beds beckoned, and they went inside. V slept badly in the sagging camp bed, trying to find a place where her shoulder, damned arthritis, didn't hurt. Her eyes itched.

IV

The next morning, V went out with her coffee to the footbridge that arched over the river near their cabin. She looked for fish, without any luck, said "Mornin" to a fisherman who was moving along the bank on the other side, and then went back in to greet Conrad, who was trying to get The *New York Times* on his phone. Phone service was wonky here; sometimes it worked, sometimes it just spun in circles. \

They breakfasted, comfortable in their quietness. V suggested that Conrad put down his useless phone and come with her to look again for fish at the bridge.

The water was clear with riffles and small waves dancing in the late morning light. The couple walked to the bridge's center, near its concrete piers.

"Hey! Oh, look – look – over there!" V pointed down river, close to where they were standing.

"Where? Where?" Conrad moved closer to her, peering over the bridge's railings.

"To the left, just above that stump, it's just a hit of pink, there's more, oh look! Look!" At that moment, a slap of fins widened into a wave that pushed against the flow of the river. 'There's more!"

Conrad stood beside her, staring intently, and then, without losing focus he stood up straighter – "I see them. I see. There are four, no five. Wow, they're swimming against the current, oops there they go, can't see them, oh there they are again."

Pink flashes showed in the water and then disappeared. Sometimes the flash was silver, a stripe, although V had trouble keeping the colors and shapes clear in her mind's eye. The pinks came and went, up almost out of the water and then hard dives back into the grays and blues and white waves. The fish were swimming hard into the stream, sometimes across the flow, avoiding the sunlight, but always part of the water's dance

V and Conrad watched, mesmerized. It was hard to keep the flipping bodies in view but just as they seemed to disappear, V would catch the edge of another murky form, flipping sideways, darting to the bottom and then up into the current. The fish sometimes turned and let the stream carry them downstream but then would face the flow again, traversing the water's heft, moving upward in and around its waves.

"Oh wow." Con's voice was soft. "They, they don't stop. They just keep going."

Eventually, Conrad's legs got tired, and V's knee ached. They limped back to the cabin, gratified. They had seen their fish. On the way to lay eggs for new life and to die. It was the first time, in all their years in the Pacific Northwest, that they had seen salmon in the wild. V felt like new life mingled with her old tired self.

Back at the cabin, weariness overtook V. She laid down on the bed and put in her eye drops. The ceiling, knotty pine, was smudged in its lines. It was good to be out here where the doctors and nurses and bad news couldn't catch them. Phone can't ring. Staff can't text. Nobody can email. All has to wait. The fish are working their way upstream. She fell asleep.

V

When V woke up and smoothed her hair, she and Conrad wandered around the grassed compound in front of the vacation cabins. A large deck for guest use jutted out over the water. A middle-aged man stood at the railing, looking idly at the stream. Conrad and V joined him.

"Seen any fish?" Conrad knew the proper conversational opening.

"No" the visitor answered. "Nothing."

"We've been coming here for years now and had never seen any fish off this deck. Or anywhere else, for that matter. I guess we get up too late or our eyes are too dim. But this morning, we actually did see some, on the footbridge, up there." Con continued the conversation.

"Oh?" The man didn't engage further, so V and Con fell silent. Upriver, on the footbridge, a little family appeared. Dad was striding at the front, all brown in his fishing gear, with a net and pole and light-colored vest. Momma's dress, bright splashes of color, blew sideways in the river-borne wind. Two small girls, bouncing and jumping as they walked, reached to grasp the woman's hands. V could hear their high-pitched chatter, although she couldn't make out the words. Dad, for that's what he must have been, walked down to the stream and waded into it until he was directly across from V and Conrad. V saw that one of the two girls, standing on the shore behind her dad, was fussing with a box attached to strap around her neck – a camera, from the shape of it. Her father swung his fishing line back and forth over the backwater.

V forgot her itchy eye and the silent fellow beside them. She loved watching the ballet of fly fishing. The young father cast his line into the dark smooth backwater they had been watching the evening before. Suddenly the rod bent in a taut arc, and the fisherman started the intricate dance of winding in and then letting the line unspool, again and again, each time bringing the line closer to the rod. V could not see the line against the green of the bank but knew from the arc of the rod that it was there.

"Sarah. Come take a picture of Daddy's fish." The young father turned and called to his daughter. Sarah came closer to the river's edge, holding her camera with both hands.

"Here. I've got it in the net. I'll turn around and you can take a photo." They could hear the man's voice over the river's burble. V was imagining that Sarah was fidgety and embarrassed. It's how she would have felt when she was that age. V squinted, trying to get the child's face to come into view.

"Here, baby, I'll bring it around. Have to keep the fish good and wet so he can breathe."

Daddy swung the fish and net upward, but Sarah still wasn't ready. Then, a tiny dip into the water again, and the father, hands dripping, reached into the net, grasped the fish with both hands, letting the net on its strap drop away.

"Quick honey, get his picture." And Sarah raised the camera. She held it and clicked. And clicked again. And again. Then the fish was lowered back into the water, where it disappeared into the river's current.

Sarah ran back to her Mom, shouting about the picture she had taken, how she had taken at least five, how Daddy had caught a really big fish. Her father patiently pulled the net to his side and reeled in and secured his line. He glanced at the three watchers across the stream.

"A good-sized bullnose," he called. "They love these dark back waters."

And he turned and waded back up to the rest of the family.

"Bull?" said the middle-aged guy next to V.

"Bull trout – bullnose – sometimes called dolly vardens," said Conrad. "They spawn in this cold stream, like salmon – are a kind of salmon or a relative or something, although they don't necessarily die after spawning. And they generally aren't colorful like traditional salmon."

Conrad had accessed Google while V had her coffee on the bridge.

"We saw them last night – they looked like otters or something – their noses and overbite go first through the water like river otters. Didn't jump any bugs, so far as we could see. Probably like the morning hatch better." Conrad did not fish, but he loved knowing things.

V looked across the river. Something strange about the experience. Charming, of course, a bit sentimental, in keeping with the clarity of the stream and the ponderosas that swayed above and even the stellar jays that added a flash of blue. But it wasn't that that she was caught by. But she couldn't think what it was.

The middle-aged man turned back toward the cabin. "Guess I'll go check out. Not much doing here," he said.

V felt indignant and then amused. Perhaps only octogenarians and children found watching fish being caught and released a big event. The river scene reminded her of Caddie and Con back in the days when they camped and hiked. The bridge children probably had stuffed animals in the car, which they would regale with tales of Daddy's heroic catch. And Daddy would earnestly explain about the release of the fish and the way the hooks were made so they didn't damage them. And Momma would listen and stroke the littlest child's hair and admire the photos on the camera's digital screen. V imagined all this and felt a bit superior to the middle-aged man, who witnessed but didn't understand.

V turned and looked down at the little inlet next to the deck. Suddenly, she recognized shapes, another fish, and then a pod of them, splashing after bugs, swimming around the small span of water, protected from the rushing stream by a log topped by swaying grass.

"Con," she called softly, not moving. "Look."

Conrad moved slowly beside her, keeping his shadow off the water. He stared at the pod of fish, which lay still against the current and then darted off, upstream or sideways or down, disappearing under the grasses or the bank below them and then reappearing downstream and swimming lazily back up.

"No salmon – not pink but…," said V.

"Rainbow trout," said Conrad. "At least that's my guess."

V screwed her eyes up to better see the fish – not the pink of the salmon nor the black of the bull trout. Speckles on gray-brown body, reddish striped and red around the head, the gills. These fish moved almost sleepily, yet could suddenly dart so fast they disappeared and you couldn't follow.

Conrad and V watched the trout until V's legs stiffened. V looked over at Con, who nodded toward the cabin. The two of them meandered back to their deck. V felt full and happy. She had never before seen that many fish, such variety, with all the darting and dancing and skating – the movement inhabited her muscles, bringing up faint memories of dancing through the night. She remembered dancing and being a young mother, and working smoothly on a college campus filled with middle-aged men who liked to drink and drive fast cars. And here she was, old and weak-eyed, thrilled by the most ordinary of cycles, fish doing what they do, families doing what they do, even middle-aged men returning to a posh resort for a massage. And she and Con, tottering back to their own quarters for grilled cheese sandwiches.

VI

As that evening drew in, V sat alone on the deck of their cabin, watching the floating bugs that filled the air. They darted in swarms here and there, reminding her of the salmon. They seemed to have no purpose, though, except maybe to feed the fish. A little like herself and Conrad, she thought, no purpose except to make up a consuming population, health care consumers, she thought. That's what we're good for.

The sun went down behind her and the trees and snowberry bushes across the way dimmed and darkened. The ponderosas and cedars were black against the lighter sky that reflected in the water. The deep blue under the small waves caught her eye again and she saw that it had indigo highlights, reflections from the waves above.

"Amazing colors," she thought. Then she looked across the stream. Against the black trees shone a world of tiny sparkling lights, not lights but illuminations, tiny things filling the air, the open space, picking up light from somewhere, bigger than dust, but not by much. It was as if the still-light sky had broken apart and was showering bits of itself down. The bits of light were white, maybe zinc white, tinged with a bit of ochre. She would use just a single strand or two-strand brush. Had to be bits of matter, not liquid, not mist, but close.

A luminous bounty, lit from within.

V had never experienced such all-encompassing light bits before. Conrad came outside and she pointed out the luminosity to him. "I think my eyes are either going or coming back."

"Swarms of bugs," said Conrad. "Making a lot of fish happy."

The lighted sky slowly dissipated. The swarming mist of tiny bugs disappeared. The evening grew dark, so dark they clutched each other's hands as they went back inside. Conrad turned on the kitchen light and got her her evening's glass of milk. Then he went back to his phone, reading about spawning salmon in the Pacific Northwest.

V sat, holding the milk. She closed one eye and looked at the edges of the glass. The edges were crystal clear, casting a sharp black outline. She closed that eye and looked through the other. It saw the glass OK, but not with the clarity of the first eye, the eye she had been putting drops into. That medicated eye saw saturated color, shimmering with the difference between the edge and the background. The colors, even in the milk, were identifiable, even maybe nameable. Or maybe not, but inside the finite space of the nameable.

She could see better.

V glanced at Conrad, wanting to share, but then said nothing and sat, closing and peering through her right eye and then her left, fascinated with the change. She glanced out the window at the now dark landscape and noticed the tinge of golden birch against the black hole of the ponderosa. The evening sky held a wash of blue in its black – Prussian blue tinged with bone black, she thought. A bit of transparency in the black.

THE REV

The Rev was round – round beard, round face, round tummy, even his legs were curved. When he talked, he held both arms out in front of him, rounded as if he were holding a big balloon. Only the furrows in his forehead and the rectangular shapes he made with his mouth were straight.

From the first time I noticed him, I figured that he was a minister. He sat in Monti's at one of the round tables, talking with earnest 20-year-olds, mostly male. The youngsters came dressed in all kinds of ways, some in tight ragged shorts, some in chinos with sharp creases. The Reverend, though, always wore a light blue, long-sleeved dress shirt with a sweater vest that rounded over his belly. He must have owned a dozen blue shirts, all alike. I figured The Rev was about 75, what with his bald head and the silver hair puffing around the edges of his ears.

When he wasn't meeting his (apparent) parishioners, The Rev drank one cup of coffee after another, and read, penciling notes along the edges of the page. He didn't look to be reading the Christian Bible – more like ancient history or some such. And I didn't know for sure that he was actually a parson – he just looked and acted the part.

The Rev seldom smiled. He stood when his kids appeared; he shook their hands, and then sat and listened to them, making his brow ridges deeper as the talk became more earnest. His voice made a quiet rumbling sound, and I never could make out the words, even though he kind of faced me.

But mostly The Rev didn't talk. He listened. The young men, who always came alone and sat with their backs toward the main café, would talk and talk, and The Rev would nod and ponder, and they (the kids) would talk some more and then lift their slumped shoulders and sit up straighter and finally thank him and reach over and shake his hand. He always stood to say good-by and then went to warm up his coffee.

Sometimes young women sat with him too, but they weren't as somber and intense. Something about his roundness made them want to tease him, to break his furrows into smiles. He remained formal and solemn with them, too, though, and then they would settle into their chairs and talk and talk and leave, looking a bit lighter after shaking The Rev's hand.

When his wife came by, it was different. The Rev would smile. A big smile. "Ah, Alyssa!" he would proclaim, as if he hadn't seen her for months.

I met Alyssa separate from the Rev – it took a month or so before I made the connection. Alyssa ran a pottery shop – a really tiny space – off a weaving studio just down Stark Street. Her shop sold mugs and dishes and china knick-knacks, stuff like that, all piled in layers on wobbly shelves that stuck out into the store's aisles. You practically had to walk sideways to get through.

The day I met Alyssa, I had wandered into her shop on my walk around the neighborhood. I hadn't checked it out before. It was winter and I had on my puffy coat and an old ragged scarf, and when I turned around to look at a set of mugs, the scarf caught the edge of a plate and the plate caught the edge of a saucer, which then jumped and overturned a cup until the whole blamed shelf tipped and everything came clattering down onto the concrete floor. And cracked and broke. Lots and lots of dishes, cups, vases, knick-knacks, all flung around my feet, in pieces.

I was shocked at the noise and then, mortified.

The owner, who turned out to be Alyssa, came out from the back room, wiping her hands. Instead of yelling at me, she opened up her arms and said "Oh wow! Are you OK? Look at that. It's glorious! Look at those beautiful shards."

She clapped her hands together and laughed out loud.

I could hardly believe my ears. There was all this broken glass, her things for sale, just lying in pieces on the floor. And she was laughing. This skinny old lady, admiring the mess on the floor and inviting me to admire it too.

Well, her reaction was classic Alyssa. Nothing bothers her much. As for the broken pottery, well, it turns out that Alyssa is an artist who makes mosaics in the back room of her shop. She loves making them – she takes broken bits of colored glass and dishes and lays them out 'til they look pretty and then sticks them into goo to keep them in place. She even sells them for table tops and vases and in frames, like pictures.

I started to say I would pay for the broken pieces and the shelf and that I was really sorry, but she just waved me off. And then she took me through the pottery mess to her back room and showed me tabletop she was working on and it was wonderful, full of colors and sparkles. I could see that all the mess in the front of the store might be useful to her. So I helped her pick up the pieces and sort them and sweep up the dust and, short version, we became friends.

The first time after that that she saw me in Monti's, she reached over the table and grabbed my hand. "I'm Alyssa, the lady with the broken glass." She smiled that big smile. "What's your name? I hope you didn't have nightmares about falling shelves and pottery pieces on your toes."

I was surprised, but shook her hand. "No, no nightmares. And Willie is what I'm called – on my birth certificate, it's Wilma. And no, I really liked what you can do with broken glass. I was glad you could get something out of the mess I made."

She sat down, and we chatted up a storm like we'd known each other forever.

Turns out she came into Monti's pretty often, for late lunch or when she closed up shop early because no one came by. She tried to avoid coming when Jimmy – The Rev – was working with his kids.

That's how I learned that The Rev – I never could call him Jimmy – was, in fact, a minister, preaching at the little church down on 89th and Davis. The Rev didn't have a degree in church stuff -- Alyssa said that he had been an engineer until he retired. They had been regular attenders at the little church when the old preacher died. The church had a money fund that took care of things like the roof and furnace and utilities, but it could only afford about $150 a month to pay their parson. So, seeing that The Rev looked and sounded the part, they asked if he would fill in.

Alyssa said The Rev had a good pension and that she made enough in the shop to pay her rent and supplies, so they didn't need the money. Alyssa said he thought about it for a long time and then said yes, he was willing to be a weekly lecturer. He said he wasn't trained, but the church board waved him off.

"I doubt Jimmy ever said no to anything if he could help," said Alyssa. "He's a pretty good preacher, too, if I do say so myself. Every Sunday he comes up with something positive to say about the world and all of us in it, and those of us in the pews go away feeling better. He keeps that church alive."

"I'm not a church-goer," I said, hurriedly. I wanted Alyssa to know that right up front that she shouldn't start in on blessings and salvation and stuff like that.

"Oh, I wouldn't be a church-goer either," said Alyssa, "except that Jimmy likes it. He likes the music – there's a ten-person choir and a neighbor who does a decent job of playing the piano. And he likes being around people, although I have to say that no one but me would know how much pleasure it gives him." Alyssa gave a little giggle.

"He has that solemn manner, all the time, and he talks slow and uses big words and so the congregation has to listen carefully to understand – if they do understand – what he is saying. But he's really good at people stuff."

Then she took a sip of her coffee and told me how The Rev settled the problem of who took care of the altar flowers.

I understood that situation because back when I was a kid, Mama and Mrs. Graves had standing battles about whether field daisies were good enough for God's presence. They argued about whose garden had the best dahlias for the vase that sat in front of the preacher's wooden stand. It just went on and on.

"See," Alyssa continued, "the church doesn't have a bathroom – a restroom, I mean, with a toilet."

Alyssa took another sip of her mimosa and eyed me to be sure I wasn't offended by the mention of private business of that sort.

"So, Jimmy combined the two issues – what to do when people had to go and how to keep the church ladies from squabbling about things that don't much matter. He said that anyone living nearby who felt safe letting their toilet be used by members of the congregation should also be in charge of the flowers. Well, after the muttering and sniffing ran its course, it turned out that Helen, who lives next to the church, has a laundry room off the back door of her house, and she doesn't mind leaving it unlocked on Sundays, 'just for us church people, you know.' "

Helen, according to Alyssa, had been important in asking The Rev to become their preacher. Helen was the church secretary. When The Rev's name came up as a possibility for their spiritual leader, well, Helen said, "Beggars can't be choosers."

Alyssa was at that meeting, and the saying became a family joke. When she asked him to do the dishes or weed the garden, The Rev would say, "OK, my dear, beggars can't be choosers," and they both would have a good laugh.

I thought the bathroom story showed that The Rev was as good as Solomon at solving problems. I also knew who Helen was. She was the woman with the loud voice who walked around the neighborhood, providing advice on plantings. She was built, as spouse Jake put it, like a Mack Truck, and wore a 1950s housedress that should have had an apron sewn onto it. She was nice enough, of course, but I could imagine her setting up a schedule for flowers that no one dared question, even if ragweed and goldenrod were her choices for an August Sunday.

And so Alyssa and I got along together. She told me the church gossip and how she wasn't cut out to be a minister's wife. I told her stories about the Monti's folks.

I got to hear how the congregation took care of its big events, funerals and weddings and high school graduations and the brouhahas that they caused. In return, I told her about Ralph and the little parties of Magdalena's lady friends. And when The Rev was through counseling and Alyssa came in, I could watch the two of them together. She would drag a chair around next to him, very close, and poke his round belly, just a light touch. If it was late enough in the afternoon, she would have a mimosa that she raised toward my table when she caught me watching.

With Alyssa, The Rev was a different man. He talked a lot, opening his books and running his fingers over lines of text. She responded with a light dancing voice, making her usual big open gestures. She was as like a needle against his tubbiness. She was older than he, although her lightness – the way she bounced as she walked and her voice, funny and trilling -- was unusual for an 78-year-old.

I always liked it when Alyssa joined The Rev. It made the whole of Monti's light up.

Before long, I knew the names of church members who sang out of key, those who only came when there was food, and who should butt out of business where they didn't belong. I felt like I could probably identify all the parishioners, even those I'd never seen. But when Morgan showed up at Monti's, I didn't know him.

Morgan was thin and nervous, looking to be about 18-years-old. He came in one afternoon, sat down with The Rev, and talked and talked. The Rev did his thing, nodding and furrowing and mumbling and then he stood up and shook Morgan's hand, and Morgan rushed out. But the next day, Morgan showed up again. The third day, he sat at another table – didn't even buy a Coke – until The Rev was through with a different young man. When that guy's hand was shook, Morgan jumped up and grabbed The Rev's hand. The Rev shook it.

"Good Afternoon, Morgan. Here you are again. What can I do for you today?" The Rev's voice was a tad sharper than his usual rumble.

Morgan sat down and dropped his head, and then lifted it, and I couldn't catch a thing he said. Even The Rev was having trouble hearing him -- once he said: "Speak up, Morgan. I can't hear what you are saying!"

Well this went on for a while and then Morgan said, fast and very loud, as if expelling the devil from his diaphragm, "I just don't know how to do it."

The Rev's round eyes got rounder. His voice got softer. I'm sure he said something like "do what?" because Morgan said, even louder and more high pitched. "It! You know -- It!"

The Rev looked down. His straight lips opened in a bit of a rectangle and then closed. And then Morgan, lowering his voice, talked and talked. And The Rev listened. Finally, he must have said it was time to go home and pray or some such, because Morgan jumped up, red-faced, shook The Rev's hand, and rushed out.

The Rev did not get another cup of coffee. Instead, he pulled out his phone. Shortly thereafter, Alyssa showed up. She didn't say anything to me, but just picked up the Rev's cup and got him a refill.

When she came back and sat down, they talked to each other, without their usual smiles. Alyssa's voice, a little excited, was just the right pitch for eavesdropping.

"He said what?" Mumble mumble.

"Oh no! Oh my gosh. What did you tell him, Jimmy?" Mumble, mumble.

"Well, this isn't exactly the place for sex ed – where were his teachers, anyway?" More mumbling.

"Oh right. Home schooling. And his parents don't allow him a personal computer – he has to use theirs so he can only watch Disney movies. And no cell phone, of course, because he's 'too young.' Damn home schooling. Yeesh!"

More mumbling.

"Oh my g… gracious. I'd forgotten – How soon is the wedding?" Alyssa's indignation had turned into concern.

"What are we going to do?"

The Rev shook his head and got up for another cup of coffee.

Alyssa looked over at me. She figured, correctly, that I had been eavesdropping.

"Poor Jimmy" she said. "He's just an engineer. No one ever asked him to be a sex counselor."

The Rev came back with coffee, sat down, and the two of them talked, now too quiet for me to hear, and then The Rev got up and went down the stairs to the antique store and I knew he was going to the bathroom because Alyssa got herself a mimosa and plunked herself down on the stool next to me.

"Oh God, young people these days. You think they've been watching porn on the internet since 2nd grade and then you find a home-schooled one who hasn't gone beyond two closed-mouth kisses and is expected to be up and horny on his wedding night. And I doubt that Grace knows much more about what to expect than he does. She's just a waif, and her mother watches her like an eagle. Why, even back in the dark ages when I was a teenager, we made out in the back seat of the car. I was technically a virgin when Jimmy and I married, but neither of us was surprised at what we found on our wedding night."

She sighed.

"I guess I can talk to Grace, although her mother's a gorgon. But Jimmy can't, I mean he can't give Morgan the lessons he needs in two weeks. Or is it three? Anyway, there's not enough time and Jimmy's not the man to do it even if there were time. And they are such sweet kids. But Jimmy says Morgan thinks he should call off the wedding because he can't do it, which makes no sense, but then whenever did young love make sense? And they've got reservations at the Plum Tree downtown, when neither one of them has ever stayed in a Motel 8."

So there was the crisis at hand, and a good one it was. The Rev came back, Alyssa grabbed him by the hand, and out the door they went, Alyssa talking non-stop.

I sat for a bit longer and then walked home. Jake and I were long experienced when we married in our 70s. And yet, here was young love, in a strange old dilemma. It practically made me misty-eyed.

The next day, The Rev came in, sat down with his book and coffee, and was joined by a young man who announced that he wanted to try out for the ministry and needed advice about what to wear. Then Alyssa came in. She seldom came in while The Rev was counseling, so her appearance startled him. But he didn't lose his formality, nodding to her as he did to me. She perched, with her mimosa, on the tall stool across from me.

"Reach up there and tear off that dance studio phone number, would you please?" she said to me.

Monti's had a bulletin board, cleaned off every Friday morning, filled up by Friday afternoon, with all kinds of services offered, phone numbers on little tags that dangled off the bottom of flyers. The one Alyssa wanted was for Jill's Dance Time, one-on-one instruction, open 7 days a week, in a pleasant family atmosphere in the home garage. Good for beginners as well as those wanting a bit of choreography for the wedding dance or salsa lessons. Reasonable rates. Close-by, in the neighborhood.

I pulled off Jill's phone number and handed it to Alyssa.

She punched in the number on her phone, turned her back on The Rev, and talked, apparently to Jill herself.

"We have a young couple who are getting married and need some dancing lessons. They're a bit shy, so my husband and I thought we would help them out. I need to talk to you, though, first, alone if possible. Can we get together soon – very soon?"

"Oh great. I'll be right down."

She shoved her untouched mimosa at me and left the Café, turning left to go down the street toward Stark. The Rev watched her, startled, and then turned back to the young wannabe, who was jolly and loud and grateful for being told to wear a suit and a blue tie. And to make sure he shook hands with the interviewers.

Then The Rev shook his hand, nodded at me, and got another cup of coffee.

I had a couple of home emergencies that kept me away from the Café for a couple of weeks. A pipe broke and Jake needed me to hold this and go after that and get the ladder and find the battery-operated whatchamacallit – things were flooding and the basement carpet was a wreck – and I had no time to wonder what was happening with Morgan and his Grace.

With all the mess to clean up, Jake and I got good and tired of one another. When we started snapping about things like hanging the ugly paintings I had bought at a yard sale, I knew it was time to go back to Monti's.

So I missed the wedding with all that lead up to it – the arguments about flowers and ribbons for the pews and music and whatnot. And I totally missed what happened with Morgan and Grace. I sat for quite a while, hoping somebody would come in so I could get the gossip. But that day I sat alone. Monti's was quiet. No church people showed up. And I finally went off home.

But then, of course, on Wednesday I came in a bit late, and there was The Rev, reading. He looked up and nodded. Later a young man came in and announced that he was going to be a lawyer and what did The Rev think about that, that plumbing didn't suit him at all. The Rev shook his hand and they sat down, and I tried to concentrate on the book I pulled off Monti's shelf about gardening in India.

Later, though, Alyssa came in. She waved at me and went over to sit beside The Rev who had finished his counseling. The two of them settled in for a bit of a giggle (Alyssa) and smiles (The Rev). Alyssa looked over at me and grinned, and The Rev nodded, with just a tiny upward twist of his mouth. When he went off to the toilet, she popped over to my table.

"Well," she announced. "We did it. Whew! I wasn't sure it would work, but it did! We did it!"

"What exactly did you do" I felt nosy about asking, but Alyssa couldn't be stopped.

"I talked to Jill the dance person – nice gal, that Jilly – and explained the situation. Morgan, well, Morgan had taken Jimmy's sermon about porn on the internet seriously, like, don't touch your girl before marriage. He worried about holding hands. Jimmy tried to explain some but Morgan didn't get it, and Jimmy couldn't deal with the details.

"Jimmy and me, back before we were married, he worried about the same problem. But I made him learn to dance, slow dance, you know, well, it can be pretty, um, interesting."

I had a quick memory of dancing with Llewelyn, my former boyfriend, the one I loved most, and I thought, oh yeah, slow dancing, now there's something.

"I remember taking his hand and putting mine in it and snuggling it up against my chest and then snuggling myself up against him, and so he got to liking dancing, and it led to other things, you know, so when the honeymoon came, we were ready. At the Steam Valley Hotel, a ways up the highway, a small room perfectly suited for slow dancing to his boom box."

She took a big gulp of the mimosa.

"It was hard, you know, telling a stranger that you wanted to bring in a couple of kids and teach them how to make out by dancing, but Jilly had a name for it: 'Intimate dancing' she called it. YouTube has some nice, not terribly naughty, videos that Jimmy and I watched. And Jilly recommended the videos to all four of us as good references on how to do the official wedding dance, and she put a link on her business card, so that made it legit. Jimmy let Morgan use his computer to watch the videos, and he and Grace started watching together.

"And then we took Morgan and Grace to Jill's garage for lessons. Jill used Jimmy and me to show what she meant – as if we were new at dancing – Jill showed Jimmy how to pull one of my shoulders toward him and put his leg between mine so our thighs touched – just so he wouldn't step on my toes, you understand – and then pull my other hand up close to him and just do a one-two, one-two, and then get a bit closer, and put his lips on my forehead and – well, really, slow dancing is nothing more than foreplay that you do in public."

I stared at her. Alyssa really understood it – that's how slow dancing worked, like before sex with someone you liked, music and the smell of aftershave, warm and close. Even Jake, when we first took up with one another, liked slow dancing.

"And it worked," Alyssa continued. "We took lessons every day for a week and a half and by the time the wedding day came around, those two had been making out like mad. You could tell just by looking at them."

She beamed at me. I beamed back. The two of us, two old ladies, thinking about making out at the prom and then afterward, in the car, in front of the house.

And back came The Rev, smiling at Alyssa and nodding, with his rectangular mouth, at me.

I couldn't shake my memories, though. When I got home, I laid the slip of paper from Jill's Dance Studio on Jake's place at the table. He saw it when he came in from mowing the grass. He read it, slowly, a couple of times, and then looked at me.

"I was thinking…" I began.

"Oh no you don't." Jake smiled and reached for my elbow. "Oh no you don't. I'm not gonna learn the salsa at age 74."

He started to pull me around toward him. I resisted.

"No changing the subject, lunkhead," I said. "Why shouldn't we take dancing lessons. We used to love it, but we haven't gone out on the town in years and years."

It hadn't really been years, but it felt like that.

"Oh honey. Oh, honey." Jake stopped holding me and frowned. He looked at the floor.

His words came out slowly. "I can't dance anymore. It makes me dizzy. When you told me about those dance lessons, I got to thinking that maybe we should go dancing again. So I tried, all by myself, in the garage last week and the room started going around and I had to sit down quick. I tried it a couple of times later, too, and the same thing happened."

He kept looking at the floor. "I just can't dance any more."

I was startled. "You didn't tell me – what if it was a heart attack or something?" I said, feeling a panic. My father died of a heart attack, and they weren't things to mess around with.

"No, no," he said, and took my phone away, laying it on the table. "The dizziness all went away pretty quick. It didn't hurt – I mean no pain, or nothing. It's happened before, like when I gardened, and nothing came of it, so I figure it's just age. But still, the truth is, I can't dance. Not anymore."

His eyes screwed up and he shook his head. I stepped up close and put my hands on both sides of his face, to stop its motion.

"We can do fun things without dancing, you goofus," I said. "We walk together and drink coffee and watch the crows," I said. "And I get to entertain you with all the goings-on at Monti's, and you tell me about all great moments in the games."

I can't stand it when I make Jake feel bad. He's a good man and shouldn't have to put up with my silly notions. It wasn't his fault he couldn't dance any more.

Although – I thought this, too, but kept it to myself – watching crows isn't like moving in a swirl, floating on air, and smelling warm-man smells and my own perfume. Coffee is good, but it isn't dancing.

Jake patted me on the back and said "Thanks, honey," and then he needed to finish cleaning up the back yard and went outside. I figured he was embarrassed by not being able to do things any more. Jake always wants to please me. He hates getting old.

I threw away Jill's number.

A week or so later I saw Morgan with a young woman – Grace. They were walking hand-in-hand down the street toward Monti's, and he reached out and stroked her bare arm. And she touched his nose with her finger. And they came in and sat down with The Rev and talked about furniture and cats. And he nodded and mumbled. And shook their hands.

WHO AM I

When Eva made her entrance with Dorothy trailing along behind, Ralph and I were sitting at the end table at Monti's. That Wednesday, he had come in, nodded at me, and sat down in the chair across from me. I hadn't invited him, but it was lunchtime and the other tables were full. It was only fair to share.

Monti's Café sits in the middle of the block at the far end of the Montabella Antique building, a big warehouse with all manner of goods – jewelry, silverware, kid's toys, clothes – brought in by vendors who have individual booths. You can walk through Montabella and up the ramp to Monti's, or you can enter the café through the courtyard at the far end of the building. That's the door that Eva and Dorothy used.

The two women stopped at a table by the window, across from us. Dorothy removed the wool cape from her mother's shoulders. She folded it, placing it on the chair next to Eva. Then she pulled out the heavy chair, so Eva, with her ramrod straight back, could sit down. Dorothy patted her mother on the shoulder and turned back toward the counter to get her tea and Eva's coffee.

Eva gave Dorothy a five dollar bill, saying "only a quarter tip, sweetheart." Dorothy turned toward us, smiling, and rolled her eyes ever so slightly.

I heard a wisp of a snort from Ralph.

Ralph and I had already sorted out our tabletop territories. We aren't what I'd call friends – mostly fellow eavesdroppers and gossips. But we rub along OK, especially since Ralph started seeing my friend Magdalena. By the time Eva and Dorothy showed up, Ralph and I had walled ourselves apart with books, drinks, and silence – minimal civilities. But Ralph is as nosy as I am, and his head now tipped slightly in the direction of the two women.

The mother and daughter seem to enjoy each other's company, even if Eva is bossy and loud. Dorothy tends to laugh at her mother's complaints about the retirement community where Eva lives, and she (Dorothy) gives Eva a rundown on her eighth graders and retired, baseball-fanatic husband. Dorothy always makes nice to people in the café; Eva, of course, ignores everyone.

I like the loud talkers – and Eva is one of them – in Monti's café. Gives me stories to take home to my ever-loving, couch-lizard spouse. I learn a lot about people and their weird lives, just by what they say at Monti's.

Dorothy returned with the coffee and tea and set the mugs on the table. "There you go, Mama," she said.

Eva picked up her coffee and tapped her finger against the mug's edge. "Disgusting."

"Mom, it's French roast" said Dorothy, sounding slightly irritated. Her tone surprised me – she's usually so pleasant. "It's OK!"

Eva held the mug away from her lips, looking at it.

"I'm talking about the cup," she said, "Not its contents."

After a sip, she put her mug down with a hard plunk. "The topic of the day, my dear, is Who Am I?" Eva often came prepared with a Topic of the Day. Ralph and I have sometimes made up our own versions of the Topic of the Day. Ralph does have a sense of humor.

After another sip of coffee Eva repeated, "I don't know who I am." Then she unwrapped her silk scarf, flinging it behind her, and unbuttoned her long, hand-knit tunic.

"Really, Dorothy, I'm at a loss. Who would you say I am, anyway? I mean, if you weren't my daughter. Knew me only as a personality. Or let me put it this way: what do you think I am – I mean, as someone you see from the outside?"

Oh dear, I thought, this conversation could go sideways. I once asked Spouse Jake who he thought I was, and I didn't like the answer.

"Oh Mama, you're my mother." Dorothy's irritation dissipated. "You are Janie's grandmother. You're Julia's great-grandmother. The kids adore you. Isn't that enough?"

Another question not to be asked. It's never enough.

"Cripes, child. No, it's not enough."

Eva's voice rose. "Is it enough that you are Herbie's wife?" she asked. She continued, "Herbie, whose only interest is keeping reams of statistics from the last Flickers game! Flickers!!! They might at least have called them 'The Vultures.' "

The Flickers are a wooden-bat baseball team in the Wild Wild West League of Portland. I know this because Spouse Jake also follows them.

Dorothy put her tea cup, which she had wrapped both hands round, on the table. She slumped back in her chair. She had heard it all before.

"Damn," said Eva, "these chairs are uncomfortable. And the table is sticky, as usual."

Dorothy shook her head, got up, and went to the counter for a clean rag. Eva looked at me. "Can't get good service anywhere these days," she said. I was startled that she knew I was watching.

I smiled and looked down at my book.

Dorothy returned and wiped off the table. She did an exaggerated scrub where her mother put her cup. Eva continued, "Anyway, dear, I'm not being melodramatic. I just don't know who I am. It's a simple fact. And I'm too old for a mid-life crisis."

Dorothy sighed, returned the rag, and sat back down. Dorothy had on baggy jeans, a Kohl's shirt, and dirty white sneakers while Eva's scarf was from a local boutique and cost more than my orthotic shoes. Dorothy was soft in the cheeks and round of belly. Eva was bony and taut. I noted that her ankles were thin, her stockings bagged a little and, underneath her stockings, varicose veins wrinkled their way into her leather shoes.

"Herbie's OK, Mama. He's got his own troubles" said Dorothy.

"Well, he's only 65, so I don't know what his troubles could be," said Eva. "He has you, for example." Eva's lips turned up a bit. "You're pretty faithful and probably wash his back."

I doubted that Eva ever washed anybody's back.

"I'm not dead yet," Eva continued. "I still need to be somebody."

Dorothy sat taller: "Now Mama! You have grandchildren. You have a great-grand. For heaven's sake, you have me. Doesn't that make you someone?"

I liked it that Dorothy spoke up for herself. That's what I tried to teach my kids, although I wasn't so good at it myself.

On the other hand, she, Dorothy, was wrong in her own way. I too have a child and a grandchild, and they are just fine as human beings go, but they aren't all there is to me. I'm a somebody, all by myself. And most of us elders have trouble figuring out who we are anymore. I took another drink of my mimosa.

"Oh Dot, of course I'm your mother, said Eva. "You air me out a couple of times a week and then check me back into 'continuing care'. They feed me gruel and lumpkins, make my bed, and check on me as I try to get out of my pants. And having a giggly grandchild and a gurgling great-grand doesn't make me somebody either."

I had often heard Eva bragging of her career as an expert on fine china, someone called on by rich people when they needed to sell their goods in a hurry. She had a real career. I had been an all-star basketball player in high school as well as the fastest checker at Safeway. But who are we – either of us – nowadays?

Dorothy shrugged. "Well, without Herb and me and the kids, who would you complain to about Paradise Acres?"

Eva made a face. "Paradise! In that place, they're all old people! "

Ralph's lips curled upward a bit underneath his mustache.

"Oh Mom come on." Suddenly Dorothy sat up straight. "You have a wonderful life. You live in a lovely apartment with all your favorite china around you. You listen to chamber music and read mysteries and play poker every Thursday. You keep up on all the latest literature about rare porcelains. You get fed gourmet meals, brought to your room when you are too tired to take the elevator to the dining room. If I were in your place, I'd be ecstatic. And you don't have to face bored and horny eighth graders every morning and a bored and not-horny husband when you get home.

Eva interrupted. "Dottie dear, I told you when you married again that you'd be sorry. Why anyone would marry a second time, I'll never know. I certainly didn't. And any male who threw his jockstrap on the floor and didn't pick it up afterward was never invited back, I'll tell you that."

Dorothy's head went up. Her chin was as high as her mother's.

Eva wasn't listening. "But who am I, that's what's bugging me. What am I doing in that, that care place, where the cups are so thick that the coffee dribbles down my front. And the place is full of walkers and old people!"

Across the table, Dorothy put her head back down, stifling a laugh.

"OK, OK," Eva continued her rant. "They take the oldest ones, the ones about to die, off to the east wing and keep their rooms dim and damp in preparation for the tomb. At least I don't have any window shades to keep out the sun, even if old Jason inches by in the morning hoping to see my boobs. But really, Dot, the place is as clean and tidy and organized as a tax collector's office. God! It smells like, like, Spic and Span."

"The place, Mama, is clean." Dorothy said, in her most patient and perhaps patronizing voice. "You hate bad smells and there aren't any. And face it, you are old, like everyone else. 83, last I counted. You have a 60-year-old daughter, who is going to retire in 3 years and 2 months who thinks she may murder her husband if she has to listen to one more mansplain about home runs and the 1950s Yankees. The statistics in that man's head…!"

Ralph was frowning; he too collected baseball statistics.

"You know what I miss?" Eva didn't hear Dorothy's problems. "I miss my papers, those boxes you kept after you sent me to the asylum. I liked looking at those papers – they reminded me of who I was – those love letters that I sent – or didn't send."

Dorothy sighed. "Oh Mommy…"

"Oh don't worry, darling, I am not going to bore you with tales of George and Sandy, although Sandy really was a sweetheart – not your type – your father was your type – but that's all gone now and so are the feelings—as well as the letters."

Eva cackled a bit, then looked fondly at Dorothy. "But you knew I was having trouble packing, and you were patient and sweet and helped me stay on track so I could be ready for the next phase of my life…" Eva's voice had become almost kind.

But of course that didn't last. Her sentence returned to today's rant – the next phase of her life "which is now, and now I don't know who I am anymore. I don't even have Sandy's descriptions of my booty to remind me. And of course, I don't have that body, either, so it's all moot." As she glanced at Dorothy, her voice softened again: "And it's OK, sweetie, really, it's OK."

"I hated it when you sold the house." Dorothy said. "It was a grand old place. Not good for someone in their 80s, but still, it was so beautiful. Herbie dotes on his nice green lawn and the cul-de-sac, but I miss the old trees – the shore pine that leaned toward the west."

"Listen Dottie," said Eva. "You did just fine – got the old house cleaned out and sold and put me into a good place where I am taken care of and they mostly hide those who are about to die. Or who are going ga-ga. But there are some real crazies there."

Eva's voice got louder. Her lips tilted upward. Ralph sat up a little. He liked Eva's tales of the old people's home.

"Old Jason, did I tell you about Old Jason? He almost got banned from the dining room the other day. He always walks around during lunch, glad-handing everyone, and he's unsteady on his feet, and last week he tipped a bit and grabbed at the nearest handle and found a female breast! Well, that could have got him sentenced to Level 4, upstairs, where you get served in your room and your minder feeds you. But the breast person forgave him and hushed up the incident, except for the gossip that we lived on for a week."

Ralph closed his book. Dorothy laughed out loud. Eva was encouraged.

"And then, the very next day, when one of the staff accidentally put on a Beatle's album, Jason started to dance. A couple of the servers went after him – what if he got tipsy again – but Alfred (have I told you about Young Alfred? – ah, a story for another time) anyway, Alfred stopped the minders who wanted to save us from unsightly obscenities – and I got up and danced with the old guy. Now that was fun!"

Dorothy was snickering. "So they aren't dead yet, eh? Not even waiting to die. Maybe I need to move to Paradise, too."

"But back to my point." Eva's said. "Who am I, anyway?

"OK Mama, let me remind you. You were, and still are, an expert on antique china – even now you get asked to appraise this cup or that vase from someone's attic. You made good money and you spent it well, on beautiful things and on your lovely granddaughter and great-granddaughter. You found yourself an elegant retirement home with silly fellow retirees, and you get to dance once in a while."

Dorothy took a sip of her tea. "So, let's face it. You are someone, even if you've forgotten. You look at your gorgeous china bowls every day. You get to rest your, your soul, in their perfection, all the time." Dorothy sighed. "But it's true that you are a person of a certain age who is living with a lot of other people just like you – making up troubles and being tiresome."

Eva changed the subject and gestured toward her now empty mug. "I wish Monti's had nice cups. But I guess no place has china cups and saucers anymore."

"Maybe you should bring your own, Ms. Mommy," said Dorothy. "You certainly have enough."

Ralph and I exchanged glances. Dorothy's voice had an edge.

"Oh, I forgot." Eva suddenly smiled. "I have something to show you."

She reached under her tunic and took out a brown lunch bag. Out of the bag, she pulled a polished octagonal wooden box with a hinged lid. Undoing the silver clasps, she slowly took out a small cup, creamy with blue figures moving along its edges. She held it in the palm of her hand. Then she turned toward the window and opened her fingers, so the light flowed through the cup and defined its shape.

Dorothy made funny noise.

"Son of a bitch." Ralph stared at the lovely object and then looked furtively around the café. "She shouldn't…. Where'd she get that?"

I looked at him. His voice was low -- only I could hear. "That looks, from here and I can't tell really tell, but that, that's a gem. Even if it's a contemporary knock-off, it's worth a bunch, and if it's real…. Oh my God. It's priceless. What's she doing with it in her pocket?"

I know nothing about fine china; in our house Corning Ware is the height of luxury. But there was something about the shape of that cup, generating its own light – it was like magic.

Eva, having lowered her voice, was talking to Dorothy. "And they don't have room yet in the nursing wing, so she's still in our wing – she's mostly in bed, you know, and her family is in and out and brings her little kitschy things from home, and one of them brought this in and set it on her dresser, and it sat there for days. The staff took to leaving her door open in case she needed emergency help when no one was with her. So I kept seeing it on her dresser and I had to check it out."

"But Mother, that's, that's… priceless. Priceless. And yes, stunning." Dorothy's voice rose. She sounded alarmed. "Even I can see that, it's so, so ethereal. But it's worth, well, you can't just…."

"I can. I did." Eva's voice was stout. "It was there, no one cared, people's stuff in nursing homes is always going missing – the staff steals it, the ga-ga people steal it, the laundry eats things. This was being treated like one more piece of kitsch like the Rosewood vase or a cat with an apple in its claws – trash that cleaning lady's dust around. I couldn't bear the thought of this, this treasure, being dusted like an ash tray."

"But Mother -- you aren't in a nursing home, you're in an expensive apartment in expensive retirement housing. People leave their doors unlocked. Nobody steals stuff there."

"Holy shit," whispered Ralph. "Grand theft."

"Oh Dorothy, I'll take it back. I will." Eva, voice lowered again, closed her hand over the cup. Holding it carefully, she put it back into its velvet-lined case. She closed the wooden lid and fastened the ornate clasps around the eight edges. She put the box back into its paper bag and slipped it into her inner tunic pocket.

Dorothy was still staring.

"I'll take it back." Eva was defensive. "I just wanted one night to look at it. It's older – it's more ancient – I never had anything like this. It holds the light. The tea is like nectar in it. I couldn't resist stroking the box, and then I took it to my room."

She stopped, looking out the window toward the sunlight.

Ralph looked up at me and shook his head: "That is so beautiful. I never thought I'd see one, so close, in that light."

He picked up my mimosa glass, tipped it toward me, "Another?" and went off to the counter. He almost touched Eva's shoulder as he walked past her.

"Come, my darling." Eva's voice turned commanding and brisk. "It's time for our stroll through the delights of the Montabella booths. Maybe the vendors have found some Pyrex for us."

Eva stood up. Dorothy, slower, got up and silently helped her mother with her scarf and cape. Eva, pulling out a beaded purse, said, "Here dear. Get yourself a mimosa. Your old Mother wants a sip or two. It cheers the vendors to see two old ladies drinking while they shop."

And then, she said, putting her hand on Dorothy's arm, "I know, I know. I can't use any more china. And you can't either. I'll put it back tonight."

Dorothy took the money and, still silent, went to the counter to buy the mimosa.

Eva looked at me. She spoke: "I really am going to put it back. I'll tell them about their cup and how valuable it is. I'll tell them tonight." she said. "I really will. But I had to share it. I needed to share it, especially with Dot."

She turned away and looked again through the Monti windows. "But now she, my Dotty, will remember me holding that cup and know I just walked in and took it. She'll remember that she had a thief for a mother."

Dorothy came back with the mimosa and set it on the table. She didn't look at her mother. Without speaking, she helped Eva with the rest of her scarves. Then they shuffled off.

"Where did you learn about china?" I asked Ralph who was standing by the table, holding our drinks.

"Oh, here and there. My job sent me around to a lot of countries, and I spent time in China and Japan. Mostly I looked at stuff because I didn't speak the language, but I read some and got better at looking and then got some ins with the traders.... Well, I guess I just learned."

Ralph reddened as he recounted that life. "I may not know who I am," he said, "but I've seen a few things."

Then he drank off his mimosa and left. I drank my mimosa slowly. I hadn't even thanked him for it.

...

I emptied my glass and started the walk home to Jake and the Portland Flickers. I didn't know if I would rat Eva out. Jake would be fascinated by her story, but I knew he would also be disturbed at Eva's stealing the cup, even if she put it back. But Eva's question, the one that turned her into a thief, that dratted "Who am I?" kept nagging at me.

"Who am I," I wondered, "Just some old lady, in her 70s, living in a small house with a tired husband, drinking mimosas and eavesdropping on other people? Who am I?"

When I got to Berrydale Park, I sat down on a bench near the basketball courts. A little girl sat across the sidewalk from me, holding a basketball in her lap. It was too big for her – she was about ten – but she was stroking its hard rubber.

She lifted up the ball, but it slipped out of her fingers and rolled toward me. I stopped it with a foot, leaned down and picked it up. It was a full-sized basketball, probably belonged to one of the players on the court. It felt good – the hard curved surface, the ridged lines. My hands still fit on the ball in just the right way.

I held it for a minute and then bounced it back at her. She caught it, and while she got her fingers around it more fully, I asked, "Do you like basketball?"

"It's Drew's ball," she said. "He's my brother. He wanted me to keep it for him – he's playing with the guys." She looked down at the ball. Then she looked at me. "I watch him play a lot – he's on the varsity team. But I'm too short to play – there's no team at my school anyway. But I like to watch. Sometime I fool around in the driveway, dribbling and shooting when he's not home. He doesn't mind me using his ball."

I gestured at her to throw the ball to me. She bounced it tentatively, and it fell short. I reached over and grabbed it.

"Good catch," she said.

I felt gust of cheer. "I used to play, in high school, a long time ago," I said. "Haven't held a basketball since Hector was a pup, but looks like I can still get my fingers around it."

"Hector?" she said.

"Oh, I just meant it was a long time ago. But I liked basketball a lot, especially playing it."

I tossed the ball to her. She grabbed it and clutched it to her chest and hung on.

"You have good-sized hands for your size," I said. "That's important. Most people don't know about hands in basketball, how important they are."

She put the ball in her lap and looked at her hands. Honestly, I couldn't tell if they were bigger than any other ten year old's, but a little encouragement couldn't hurt.

She picked up the ball and threw it at me, a little harder. I caught it and threw it back. We sat there, sometimes bouncing, sometimes tossing the ball back and forth. She asked me what position I played. "Forward," I said. I told her that I liked teamwork more than scoring points.

So we chatted for a while and then the boys finished up their game and her brother came over. I tossed her the ball one last time and got up and left.

I had been a basketball player in high school. Got offered a sports scholarship to the local teacher's college but couldn't use it. I knew when I had made a good pass. I could still feel it, and it felt good.

Like Ralph, I had seen a thing or two, even if I didn't have the right answer to that dratted question.

KINWORK

The Ordering of Bulbs: Late May

Late May in Portland, Oregon. Trees drape over sidewalks, dank with yesterday's rain. Bushes hang low, showering dogs and making diamond lights in their eyelashes. The world is heavy, dark with limp green leaves and water-stained concrete. May in Portland is wet, dank, chilly -- and full of blooms.

Caddie parks under the dripping ash tree and stares absently at the yard beside the car. The small suburban lawn is stuffed with shrubbery and flowering plants – forsythia, lilac, hydrangea, beauty bush, brunnera, columbine. Amid them are the stubby remains of tulips and daffodils.

Caddie sighs. Her elderly mother is in a twitch. Conrad sent Caddie a text, and she has come.

She slowly gets out of the car.

V (Valentine on her birth certificate) is at the dining room table, brochures and scribbled papers surrounding her laptop. Her fingers are pushing into her tangled hair. Her elbows are sunk into heaped notecards. She glances at the door.

"Calendula, my dear. Here you are. It's May again." V is in one of her dramatic moods. She is an octogenarian enthusiast who immerses herself in projects and pulls everyone else into the maelstrom.

"Tulip ordering, right?" Caddie smiles at her mother.

Caddie had been forewarned. V must order next year's spring-blooming bulbs – tulips, daffodils, crocuses and allium. But she is stuck. Has been stuck for weeks. Nursery catalogues lie in piles, and notepapers fly every which way when the front door opens. Next year's bulbs must be ordered at the end of this year's bloom. It happens at the same time, every year.

When V was younger, she had found the May deadline useful. But time has shortened both her spine and her decision-making capacity. Her executive functioning has slowed; the variables of flowering bulbs has increased. She's stuck. But it is almost June, and the bulb order must be completed

"Tulips. Daffodils. Hyacinths. Crocuses – oh my God, the crocuses! Do you know how many new versions of crocus there are? And then there's allium, freesia, anemone, *fritillaria meleagris*. Tulips!" V's voice rises.

"There are lily tulips and peony tulips and tulips that look like space ships! There are even tulips that look like tulips!"

V, an oil painter of exuberant shapes and colors and buttery textures, has painterly flower beds on every inch of her city property. Her gardens are another version of her paintings. And her tulips are her *magnum opus*, a neighborhood event, demanding the artist's attention and urgency. But she is feeling the bafflement of age.

Caddie, behind her mother's seat, tugs gently at V's hair.

"So what's the problem, Mama? An excess of joys? Too many choices? Tulip mania?"

"Oh Caddie." V looks around at her 60-year-old daughter.

"Don't be sarcastic. You make me sound like a muddled teenager. You're just as bad about asparagus and onions."

"Now, Mama, I'm only making a little fun," says Caddie. "you'll survive. Every year you pull your hair out and then decide to spend a lot of money and make gigantic orders that boggle the mind. You could feed a small country on what you spend on tulips."

This is Caddie's usual comment about V's extravagant bulb plantings. Caddie prefers food crops.

In practicality about gardening, Caddie resembles V's deceased cousin. Nora also believed in vegetables. Nora died two years before, but both V and Caddie still hear her saying "What a waste of perfectly good dirt!" Caddie agreed.

V argued.

"The tulips, my dear," says V to Caddie, "are essential. They fulfill their destiny. They bloom to bring pleasure – enormous pleasure -- even to cabbage-minded people like yourself."

Caddie rolls her eyes. Conrad winks at her.

"Anyway," V's voice gets brisk. "No time for the old arguments. I'm drowning in how to avoid last year's muddle when I got all late bloomers and thought nothing was going to bloom, which it didn't until late April, by which time I'd given up and started to plant annuals and then I found all those bulbs sprouting where I had planned to put more phlox. The year before that the squirrels took bites out of 78 percent of the bulbs I planted. They didn't even eat them – they just bit them."

"She's been like this for a week, Caddie, so she's almost at the end." Conrad had thrown his daughter a kiss when she came in and then gone back to reading *the Times*. But he is listening.

"Well, that's good to hear." Caddie grins at her father. "Come on, Mama, where are you lost now?"

Caddie loves her mother. And even her mother's flowers.

"OK, let's hear it," she said. "What themes are you thinking of? Color? Shape? Weird or methodical? Linear or circular? Early or mid or late? What's this year's scheme?"

V perks up. She has thought about her intentions.

"This year, I'm going everywhere. Mixed color, randomly planted. Early, mid, and late blooms. No peony look-alikes, but definitely the lily flowers and the parrots – lots of them. Some tall red classics for the upper boxes. A *few* dark purples."

Caddie nods. Cross out the doubles that look like peonies and most of the "dark emperors" and "black spiders." That only leaves a thousand or so colors and shapes and sizes.

"I've made some lists" – V nods at one of the piles of scrawled papers, "but I got lost in them."

Suddenly she looks down. Her voice trails away.

She adds: "Maybe I'll just write an essay about tulips."

Writing essays – or talking about writing essays – is V's base distraction strategy.

Caddie looks at her mother. "You're procrastinating," she says. "First you need to do the ordering. Then you can daydream. So, to work."

Caddie pulls a chair around and inserts a thumb drive into V's laptop. "I've brought my vegetable template. We'll change the categories, pull in the variables and input what looks good. The computer can tell us how many of each to order. OK?"

V looks at Caddie. "You can do that?"

Conrad says, from the living room: "I bet AI would do it even faster."

V thinks to take up the subject of AI and its potential for destroying civilization, but a look at Caddie keeps her mouth shut. She'll let Caddie make the lists; she can always change them later.

And so the two women work together, murmuring, laughing at tulip names: La Belle Epoque, Black Hero, Yellow Pomponette – and discuss naming new varieties: Fagan, Noddy Boffin, and Barkis (who would be willing to bloom even when squirrel-bitten). They discuss new shapes they think should be bred: squat chamber pots are V's favorite, while Caddie lingers over toasters. By the time Caddie leaves, the order is done, and V settles by the gas fire. Conrad smiles at her. Another year's abyss, navigated.

"What a lovely daughter we have," V says to Conrad. "Maybe next year she can do the whole order herself."

Conrad grins. "Well, alliums are just a fancy garlic, so she'd be OK with that. But you won't get any tulips."

"Maybe I'll get run over by a truck and won't care."

This is V's standard joke when faced with future difficulties.

They sit back, listening to the spring rain, and V revels in the thought of the spreadsheet.

The History of Help: November

"Maybe I'll write an essay about planting tulips."

V looks over at Conrad, who is absorbed in the NY Times column about climate change and fall hurricanes.

Conrad looks up. "That sounds, um, interesting. What about planting the tulips? Isn't it about time? Have you scheduled our diggers yet?"

V has always been the family gardener, pulling out unsightly vagrants, and with Conrad's help, planting new finds from distant nurseries. But these years, neither V's hips nor Conrad's knees bend or kneel readily. They both suffer from vertigo. So, while they sometimes imagine they could plant six or eight hundred bulbs, they can't. Help is needed, which means V has to get her gardeners scheduled.

Again V hears Nora's voice, chiding her for wasting money. Nora worked as a home health aid until she was 80. She grew geraniums in pots – and V, in her mind, reminded Nora that she, V, didn't grow geraniums.

"Too easy," V would say to herself. Besides, hiring gardeners gives V many tales to tell, something even Nora approved of.

V loves telling tales.

"Gardeners These Days" (that's the way her stories start) are a varied lot. At first, V hired one of the college-student waiters from their favorite café. Christine had good intentions but had never gardened. She scraped at the soil and looked blank when V showed her how to use a shovel. The two of them agreed that Christine was a great people-person who served wonderful coffee -- and parted cheerfully.

Then V requested recommendations from her garden chat group, which resulted in 16-year-old Percy, driven to the house by his mother. Percy was a magnificent digger, who shoveled and planted the front bed under her supervision and her patient listening.

Percy talked and talked and talked as he shoveled clay and laid down compost. His subjects were his high school problems, his single mom, his GED attempts. V was relieved when he got a full time job at Walgreens.

V's last failure was the spendy professional outfit. The service claimed expertise in every kind of garden, but the men who showed wanted to rototill, leaf blow, and clear out blackberries. They had never planted bulbs. After she and Conrad replanted, in the November rain, 650 tulip and daffodil bulbs that the landscaping guys left sticking out of the ground, V almost gave up salvaging spring from its gloom.

"No more tulips," she announced. And Conrad nodded, in silence, aware of his aching back, his love of the spring flowers, and V's inconsistent proclamations.

And of course, the following spring, the brilliance of garden color in the midst of dingy March annihilated V's resolve. At the end of May she embarked, once again, on decisions about daffs and fritillaria and parrot tulips.

That was the year that Aggie showed up, wondering if, given the number of flowers and plants and bulbs that she, Aggie, had seen in the gardens, if she, V, could use some help. Aggie admired an exotic hebe and gained V's instant approval. V was over the moon when Aggie pooh-poohed Conrad's offer to shovel. Aggie planted as V intended rather than as V instructed. Aggie was the gardener V had always dreamed of, coequal -- and younger.

However, Aggie, just when the bulbs need planting, became home bound with bronchitis. The bulbs now sit in their boxes in the garage. Smaller bulbs, a hundred or so, have been planted by Alejandro beside the driveway, but the majority of bulbs, 600 or so, are still waiting.

Conrad tilts his head. "*We* aren't going to plant the tulips, are we? I mean, Alejandro is coming, right? You texted him, right?"

Conrad's voice rises just a little.

V sighs. She hasn't texted Alejandro. She yearns for Aggie. Aggie knows the garden and has small feet. She crawls under the rosebushes. When V is vague, Aggie becomes decisive. The garden is a canvas, and Aggie is the artist's assistant who can read her mind. She and V are simpatico.

Alejandro, V's back-up garden person, is good in different ways than Aggie. He handles large shrubs easily and enjoys fixing rotted wood. He can put in a row of hebes with precision. He loves roses. But he is bigger than Aggie and has trouble fitting under low bushes. And Alejandro's other job is with a landscaping business, run by an accountant who lays out the exact order and spacing of each azalea and boxwood hedge plant, relying, so V imagines, on making money. V refuses to think how much her bulbs cost.

Alejandro appreciates V's gardens when they bloom. But her rapid speech and ever-changing planting instructions bemuse him. Alejandro is quick to learn and puts up with V's flighty directions. But he has never worked with 600 bulbs in late November.

V texts Alejandro, who agrees to come on Tuesday, the only day he has from his full-time job.

After V closes down her phone, Conrad reminds her that the golden ash, their beloved tree that overhangs the front tulip bed, is to be trimmed on Tuesday.

V narrows her eyes and says she and Alejandro will work around the arborists. Conrad says he will be at his computer if they need him.

The Planting of Bulbs: November

On Tuesday the drizzle stops at 4 AM and the temperature starts to rise. The threadleaf coreopsis, large and mounded, is in its autumn glory, lime-green yellow topped by deep matte burgundy. And the beauty bush's leaves blaze gold in the midst of the waiting tulip bed.

V is re-sorting the bulbs on the floor of the front porch, waiting for Alejandro's arrival. The bulbs, varying sizes, feel alive to V's finger tips. Daffodil bulbs are rough and knobby and anemones are small nuts that are soaked before planting. But the tulips are covered with paper-thin, red-brown skins that slide off their tear-drop shapes which are cool, smooth, and creamy. Fondling the bare tulip bulbs feels like touching precious gems. Their roots are tiny and tender, their tips stout and upward perking. V loves holding all bulbs, but her greatest pleasure is in the tulips.

V takes a deep breath. She tells herself to be clear and simple while instructing Alejandro. She frets about whether she should put more yellows with the plumbago, which grows slow and late. But when Alejandro's truck pulls up, she forgets her worries. He waves and smiles. He pulls out tools from the back of his truck and comes to the porch to look at the bulbs.

"Ah, you are planting a lot of bulbs." Alejandro observes. "Are these all for the front yard?"

"Well, mostly. Some will go in the planter boxes and some in the back, along the wall. But we'll do the front first and then see what we have left. Oh and we have to save some bulbs for Laura, across the street. And for the pots on the back deck. And maybe…." By that time Alejandro has moved to the porch and is reading the labels V has laid over the piles of bulbs.

Marge, from next door, wanders over to stand in front of the porch.

"Hey, V, what's up? Tulip planting? I have to get some in myself – just been so wet I couldn't bring myself to do it."

Marge is V's favorite temptress. It is Marge who talks her into buying one more rose bush and yet more hydrangeas. V encourages Marge to put in more bulbs.

"Aggie is sick, so Alejandro is filling in," says V. "Thank heavens for the dry day."

V knew Marge wondered why Alejandro and not Aggie. Marge keeps an eye on the neighborhood.

Just as Alejandro has gotten the tools arranged and the first bulb into the soil, Jasper, the tree guy, and his crew appear. V explains about the bulb planting under the ash tree's wide branches. Jasper turns to Alejandro. The two of them strategize on keeping out of each other's way. V fusses at Alejandro about falling tree branches. Alejandro smiles and tells her he will plant in the south while Jasper prunes to the north. Then they will trade places.

"They are very good at lowering the branches," says Alejandro. "They won't kill your bushes."

"And not my gardener either," says V, only half kidding.

"They are very good." Alejandro says again, nodding at the equipment Jasper is putting beside the tree trunk. "They know what they are doing."

"Could you do tree work like that?" V imagines Alejandro, roped in, dangling from a mammoth fir.

"Oh no, no, no." Alejandro grins at her and puts his hands out in front of him, wagging them back and forth. "I get scared. My legs jiggle. I would fall off."

V remembers climbing trees, back in the tiny village she grew up in. Climbing trees and stealing cherries with her cousin Nora. A sliver of homesickness twists inside V, and she remembers that Nora is dead and she is 85 and neither will climb a tree again.

Alejandro laughs and gestures to the bulbs on the porch. "Shall we begin?"

V tosses the bulbs onto the soil, showing rather than telling Alejandro how to space them. He nods and moves some that he thinks are too close together.

V watches Alejandro put in the bulbs. He uses a simple trowel, digging firmly through clay and roots. As V watches him work, her left hip starts to sag and hurt. Conrad, who had come out to check on the chainsaw progress, sees V's crooked posture. He gets a lawn chair for her, sitting it on the sidewalk beside her with a touch and a smile. Jasper and his crew shout instructions and jokes back and forth, and Alejandro joins in. V relaxes, although when a large branch swings from the tree, she makes high-pitched sound.

"They know what they are doing," repeats Alejandro, from his spot in the tulip bed. And he is right. The branch is lowered to the sidewalk, 20 feet from where Alejandro is digging his holes. By the time the tree workers are ready to move to the south, Alejandro has put in the compost and bulb food and is ready to plant the north end of the bed. V watches as his long fingers work the trowel, his palms adding strength.

"Oh to be 50 again," she thinks.

When he stands up, he stretches his back and nods at her. "It's going to be beautiful." He gestures across the newly planted earth.

Jasper's crew has moved on to the branches overhanging the street, leaving the front clear for Alejandro.

"And now for the chicken wire," says V.

Alejandro frowns. He thought he was finished.

"The squirrels," says V. "The squirrels dig up the bulbs. They don't eat them but they take bites out of them. Or maybe it's the rats or crows – I don't know, but the bulbs don't do well when something eats at them. So – chicken wire."

Alejandro looks at this talkative woman, with her wild hair and her shrunken figure. He smiles, and V realizes he has no idea what she is talking about. She stands up from the lawn chair, and walks to the back of the studio. Alejandro follows and sees the heap of pointy chicken wire. He nods. "Ah, yes," he says.

Cutting and laying down the chicken wire over the planted bulbs and around the various shrubs and bushes takes another hour. By the end, Alejandro looks weary and V is speechless with fatigue. Jasper explains how the tree is looking good and will weather the winter storms. Conrad pays Jasper, and the arborist and his helpers feed the branches into the chipper, bagging up the debris. Alejandro looks with approval at the tidiness of the gardens and walks and nods with pleasure.

"It's going to be beautiful," he says.

The First Blooms: Early March

And, in its own slow unfolding, it is beautiful. February ice storms come early and merely frost the daffodil tips. The squirrels aren't able to dislodge the chicken wire. The first wild iris blooms along the far side of the driveway, and the daffodil spears come on green and fast. The tulips poke up their green noses in earnest. The crocuses, with their purples and yellows, come and go, giving the neighborhood a taste of the color to come.

V reminds herself to order more crocuses for next year. Elaine, from around the corner, comes up the driveway examining the beds. She asks about the newly blooming, multi-colored flowers that line the pavement.

"Anemone. New this year," said V, bending down to pull some dead foliage. "Don't know if they'll work or not."

Elaine nods. "You never quite do, do you, in gardening. Nor in life either." She walks on down the street.

Elaine needs color, thinks V.

Marge comes over with her husband, Lucas, and checks out the planter boxes Alejandro rebuilt last year.

"Nice job," says Lucas.

Marge inspects the deep purple flowers just coming into bloom. "Almost as Black as me," she says.

"We tried," said V. "But the growers aren't very helpful."

The two women grin at one another.

Marge moves on to the flowers lining the driveway.

"Yeah," said V, imagining Marge was seeing some bare soil. "Those are a little sparse – next year I'll have to have more small bulbs. And the anemones might spread."

Marge laughs. "Oh yeah, they'll spread. They'll eat your car."

Marge makes V laugh.

Aggie drives up, rolls down her window, and shouts "Looking good," and drives off. Laura, from across the street, shouts to V that the bulbs she has given them are starting to bloom. Patrick, whose bedroom windows overlook the ash, comes by. "Looks OK this year. Branches startin' to get gold. Your arborists must have been OK."

Alejandro comes by after work. He checks his plantings, notes where the squirrels have tunneled under the chicken wire, and finds a big rock to prevent their further intrusion. Caddie calls to see how spring is progressing and to report on her dandelions and lettuce.

Spring has sprung.

The Fullness of Flowering: April

As the weather grows warmer, more people stroll or run by the gardens. The Asian-American guy who walks three tiny dogs keeps their skittering paws away from the mass of blooms. He smiles big when he sees V watching. The toddler from down the street pulls up a tulip by its top and offers it to his mother. The mom, spotting V and Conrad at their front window, apologizes, making a face. V waves and forms a heart sign with her hands. An old woman, a member of the tiny church near

Monti's, stout and grim-faced, slows her stride to examine the yellow tulips more intently.

"I bet she's remembering her tulips at the county fair 40 years ago," remarks V to Con, who grins at her. "Hers were bigger, brighter, and more plentiful, for sure."

Pilar, a new grandmother comes by, and V goes out to poke at the toes of the baby she is holding. V loves the way babies feel and smell. She doesn't get a chance to adore tiny ones very often.

"Here, have a bundle" Pilar says, handing the baby to V. V cuddles the sweet warmth and remembers the luscious sensations of life -- flesh that fits perfectly in one's arms.

"Such a treat," she says to Pilar, "Thank you."

Pilar nods in agreement. The baby starts to squirm, and V hands her back to her grandma.

A phone-reading woman walks by, preceded by a large dog who jumps into the bulb bed and starts to squat. V and Pilar shout, simultaneously, "Stop!"

The dog's owner, startled, looks up, and tugs the dog out of the flowers. The dog yelps and wraps itself around the woman's legs. V has a surge of rage, and then finds herself laughing out loud as the leash gets tangled around the woman's legs. The woman apologizes, sulking, and yanks at the dog. V waves her off.

Pilar says to V, "you're remarkably charitable. I'da killed her."

"No you wouldn't have. But I appreciate the thought." V has a swoosh of pleasure from Pilar's support and how the bundle of baby felt. Even the thought of dog and woman tangled together made her glow a little.

"Cousin Nora," thinks V "would have liked Pilar."

She imagines the late bulbs growing upward in the warm soil as their roots squirm into soft earth.

A Time for Beauty

One evening in early May, when the late blooming tulips, always the tallest, are festooning the yard with color, V, Caddie, and Conrad sit on the front porch. The Sweet Sunshine clematis is starting to wind its way around the porch railings. The air is balmy and dry.

"How did this year's crop do?" asks Caddie.

"Well, the colors aren't quite like the online photos, and the shapes didn't balance as I imagined. And we ended up with some really dark purples – I think I got them from Bluestone on sale."

V's critique is expected by both daughter and husband.

"But they're good enough," she adds. Caddie smiles.

During the rains, V had seen the golds and burgundies of the early flowers made brilliant by the backing of luminous gray skies and scattered mists. Now the evening sun of late spring catches the tips of the tallest flowers, making them glow. The deep purples are unspooling, contrasting with the lime green of new rose and hydrangea foliage.

A car drives by slowly and then stops across from the house. It's the church lady again. The three on the porch watch as she gets out and walks around the car, not seeing the porch sitters.

In her flowered house dress she echoes the flowering garden. She scans the growing plants, slowly, deliberately. In this light, her portliness turns regal; she looks like a goddess. She walks from one end of the bed to the other, and then turns and walks back again.

Finishing her tour, she moves to a circle of Blushing Beauties and Lambada tulips and stoops to examine them more closely. As she stands upright, she catches sight of the three people on the porch, watching her.

She looks at them for a minute, and then she smiles. She raises her hands, palms upward, and gestures over the field of color and light.

"Glory be!" she calls in a rich contralto. "A time for beauty. Yes, Lord, a time for beauty."

Conrad looks at her fine upright body, backing the colors, being enveloped by them, yet more solid and real.

"Glory be," he yells and gives her thumbs up. Caddie raises both her arms, palms turned upward. V beams and waves wildly.

The woman repeats, "A time for beauty," and with one last sweep of the garden, she turns and walks to her car.

PLACING MOM

Monti's was quieter than usual that day. Only Magdalena's crew, at the far end of the café, discussed shoes over their mimosas. I was sitting with my usual coffee and mimosa. Spouse Jake was at home, watching basketball. He always was puzzled when I decided to pass up the afternoon session.

"But Willy," he'd say, "The Ospreys are battling the Gypsums for first place! This is the crucial game. You can't miss it."

I, Willy, could miss it. And so here I was, listening to a melodrama at Monti's. Two women – ones who came around a lot – came into the café dining room.

Sisters -- definitely. They even finished each other's sentences sometimes. And they knew all kinds of family stories, which gave me good eavesdropping days.

Today, though, they looked drawn and tense. Both stood next to me, not seeing me, putting their gloves on the vacant table across the way. The smaller one spoke in a quiet voice, while the big one was loud and sharp. A looming family crisis, perhaps.

The women looked to be in their 70s. The quiet one had a round face, was thin and held herself in tightly, as if trying to vanish. The louder one was not just bigger – taller and fatter, taking up more space – but she had strong lines around her mouth that gave her a formidable look. They talked in low, tense voices. I had to strain to listen.

"We have to find a place to put her!" Small sister put her cup down, the string from the teabag hanging over the edge and stood still, only her hands moving. She was grabbing her fingers and pulling at them. She sat down on the front edge of the wooden chair, perched, ready to fly off.

The older woman, hair falling forward around her thin lips, flicked her fingers at her sister. She plunked herself into her chair, filling up the seat and shoving her rear to the back. She set her coffee down with a thump.

"Really Maud, at least you could say 'place her'" she said. "It sounds like you want to put a dog away."

She made a snorting sound.

"Sheryl! You mean thing," said Maud. "You know I don't mean that, I mean … I mean, we just have to put her somewhere safe." Maud's voice was high and tearful.

"There you go again. Putting her away." Sheryl took a swig of her coffee. "Besides, Mama won't go. She isn't a tabby cat that you can pick up and cage. She'd fight like a Siberian tiger!"

"Sheryl!" Maud wasn't conceding, even as her voice wavered and dropped off.

I glanced over. Maud was dunking her tea bag furiously, splashing the liquid on the table.

"Oh, Maud, for pete's sake. Here. Let me wipe you up before you get your sleeve wet." Sheryl used a paper napkin to wipe up the spilled tea.

The day's drama was set.

The two women came to Monti's frequently. Sometimes they were with an old lady, I mean, a really old lady. It seemed like an outing, a treat for the threesome. The sisters treated the old woman as if she were a tiny doll, unwrapping her from three or four outer coats and sweaters while she protested and laughed. They were comical; Mama trying to wiggle her way out of her own coats, and Maud and Sheryl grabbing and untangling them and smoothing down various other parts of Mama's clothing that got pulled up by the struggles. Mama always dominated the conversations, while Maud and Sheryl murmured or shouted (Mama's hearing wasn't very good) and got her a cookie that she crumbled over the table top. She scolded them, they laughed, she laughed, it was all very jolly.

But it wasn't jolly today.

"It was awful -- the Walkers called and said she was at their house without any clothes on – I didn't know she had gotten out of bed. It was like, 3 a.m. I ran right over and they kept looking away from us, like up at the sky, telling me how she banged on their door and scared the dog. The dog was still inside, barking like he'd like to take Mama's leg off."

Maud's voice rose, remembering the scene. "I had to talk Mama into coming home – she kept insisting that she needed to get into her house – she meant the Walkers' house -- to clean up after the dog. It took us an hour of coaxing for her to go back home with me. Naked the whole time, even though it was about 50 degrees. Mrs. Walker ran in and got her a blanket, but we had a hard time keeping it on."

"How'd she get out?" Sheryl asked.

"Don't know. I have to keep the key in the big door --otherwise I keep losing it. But I hooked the screen door and she can't reach the hook -- or at least I didn't think she could." Maud sighed. "It was unhooked when the Walkers called, so I guess...."

So Mama was living with Maud. Poor thing.

"Maybe Mama found a tool! Like an old crow!" said Sheryl.

Sheryl snorted; Maud grinned, just a little.

"But what are we gonna do?" Maud sounded helpless, in front of a wall that refused to move. She was desperate for Sheryl's advice. Older sister Sheryl could move mountains.

"How about another hook? Higher up? Tom could bring over his drill?" Sheryl asked.

"I can barely reach the one that's there now," said Maud. "And if Mama can get at that one, she can reach anything that I can."

"We could have the locksmith over and install a bolt that locks and you could sleep with the lock on a chain around your neck." Sheryl's problem solving voice softened a bit.

Maud was wringing her hands again. I hoped she didn't have arthritis. My pinkie finger could never have stood all that pushing and shoving.

"But what about fires? What if we couldn't get out?" Then Maud grabbed her tea cup with both hands. "Oh Sheryl, I can't do this anymore."

Sheryl waved her hand and then got up and came back with a couple of mimosas. Maud sat curled, stonelike, her hands still wrapped around her undrunk tea.

"Well, I guess Tom and I could have her again," said Sheryl slowly. "I know how hard it is, how crazy-making. I was frantic every hour of the day. When she started getting out of our house, we kept working on the door she used – and then she would go on to the next one. She found ways to get out of all five of them, especially at night. And during the day whenever anyone came in and didn't carefully lock behind themselves, out she would fly. Damn, she's in incredibly good shape for an old crow."

Maud shook her head. "All she wants is to go home."

Sheryl's voice got snippy. "And of course, she is 'home', in the old house that you got when you were first married and had Melissa, and Gus was down on his luck" – I had heard about Gus's "luck" before – seems Maud was lucky to have divorced him before it really got bad –

"And" Sheryl said, flicking her thumbs out in mock disbelief, "she still wants to go home."

Maud shook her head. "I guess she wants to go back to when she knew what was happening and could tell us off and help people out and bake cookies."

They sipped their mimosas. Maud looked defeated, Sheryl defiant. Two ways to face the inexorable, written on their faces.

"Do you think Johnny, you know, Melissa's Johnny, would spend some time with you? He could sleep in the living room?"

Sheryl was working on the problem. "Johnny's a night owl and he would hear her if she tried to get out. And Melissa said he's at loose ends right now."

Maud held her mimosa glass tightly by its frail stem. "It would be awful to have an eighteen-year-old guy hanging around all night. And what would I do with him during the day? And he would want me to feed him!"

This was a common discussion between the two. It seems that Maud ate cereal and fed Mama cereal for almost every meal. Sheryl took meaty casseroles to them at least five times a week.

"I don't know why you don't just cook. It can be fun – you used to like it. You could start up again."

Maud sat up. "We aren't going to get into all that. That's it. That's all. And I never asked you to bring any food; you know I was figuring out how to get Melissa to order out for me, but no, you took it on yourself, bringing over those dishes that I have to wash up, so don't give me any talk about cooking."

Oh dear. I was beginning to wish I was down in the doll aisle of the antique store. I don't cook either.

"Come on, Maud, it's OK, it's OK." Sheryl reached over and touched Maud's hands. "I don't mind bringing food, and really, you don't have to wash the dish. It won't hurt it to sit 'til I pick it up. I have lots of casserole dishes."

Sheryl did seem the type to have matched casseroles, with the extras stored in the basement.

"And if I need any more," she said, "well, there's lots in the collectibles in the antique store. They sometimes have real antiques, interesting shapes and sizes that I don't have."

Maud sat back a little. "Antiques with lead, I'm sure," she said and sipped from her mimosa.

Sheryl ignored her.

Maud conceded. "Well, maybe Melissa's Johnny would like to get away from his mother a bit. But Sheryl, what'll he think when Mama takes off her nightgown to watch TV?"

Sheryl snorted –she really had that sound down -- and they both sat silent for a bit.

"Well," said Sheryl, "I'll have Tom put in another hook on the screen door – maybe way down low. Maybe she won't be able to figure that out." They both shook their heads.

Something would have to be done. Or something would turn up.

The two sisters gathered up their things, swigged the last of their mimosas, and went outside. Sheryl was parked at the curb, and I watched as they said good-by and she got into her van. Then, after sitting for a minute, she put her head down on her steering wheel. Maud, who had started down the street toward her Toyota, came back and knocked on the side window. She crawled into the van.

I went to look at the wedding dresses for collectible dolls. I couldn't bear to watch them, still talking.

THE PALOUSE

I

"Ouch! Damn! Damn, damn, damn!" V leaned over and glared at her big toe, stubbed on the table leg. "Fuck!"

She glanced at Conrad at the end of the table, who said, in his quiet way, "Language, m'dear, language."

Conrad had been dead three years, three months, and seventeen days, but he still spoke to her at breakfast. Sixty-odd years of marriage had branded his looks and mannerisms into V's physical and mental systems. V could see him now, making sure her injuries were minor and smiling at the naughty words.

Sitting down with her coffee – which had spilled onto her fingers when she stubbed her toe – she pondered obscenities.

"I wonder how kids today swear – do they still use excrement and sex and private parts?" She wiped her hands on the table napkin. She did not say this out loud. Conrad was, after all, still dead.

Dammit.

V had been unsettled even before the table leg rose in front of her toe. She had awakened from a bad dream just as it was getting light on this late spring morning. She wouldn't recount the nightmare to Conrad. Too long and boring to tell a dead man. But she couldn't get the black figures out of her brain. The most horrifying figure, whose all-black clothes had razor-sharp edges, had been slicing away at Conrad's favorite daphne bush beside their front stoop.

An ugly dream. Probably about death. Or painting. Or Conrad. Or about *New York Times* stories of scams and elderly people being murdered by men with gardening tools.

It was hard being old this morning. And then there was the stupid Times caption:

"The caption on this photo is stupid." She spoke to the empty chair where Conrad used to sit.

V looked back at the article about a spendy resort on a distant Pacific Island. The column, in the "Travels" section of the paper, was preceded by a photo of an elegant breakfast table -- immaculate white cloth with indigo blue napkins, bright orange juice, and steamy coffee in fine translucent china with willow images that wafted down the sides of the cup. A golden croissant was laid out next to heavy cutlery and glasses. The table and two chairs sat in front of arched, ceiling-high windows through which blue skies and green nature were framed. Everything was flooded by warm light.

The view from the windows was of a formal garden with evergreens cut into nymph shapes, romping among the dahlias. Beyond the garden was a viridian-green forest and in the far distance, a tiny white triangle, presumably a mountain, topped with that strip of blue sky.

The caption below the photo read: "Volcano looms over ritzy resort".

What actually loomed in the photo were the orange juices in heavy glassware, the beautiful blue lines on the saucers, and the buttery croissants.

Conrad said, "Looks like great croissants. And Mexican coffee – yum."

"The article says the volcano is smoking," said V, "but it's just a white blob in the photo. Maybe the management bribed it to stay dormant."

She sighed to herself. It was a morning thing – these conversations. She only talked out loud to Conrad at the table, where she could imagine his fuzzy-white hair backlit against the sun streaming through the windows.

She had gotten up on the wrong side of the bed. It irritated her that Conrad was dead. Her back ached and her shoulders pinched with arthritis. And in *The Times* photo, the volcano neither loomed nor smoked. It was merely a prop.

"Arrest them for language misuse," she thought snarkily. Conrad's imagined form had disappeared. "I wonder if there is a right side of the bed."

V was a painter, aged 89, who had disposed of most of her inventory – those 6-foot by 6-foot landscapes – by giving the painted canvases to young artists who scraped and sanded off her images, painting over them. Friends thought she should have a big sale, an auction, to diminish her inventory. She thought with horror -- such an exposure of her life's work could be humiliating. What if no one bought anything? What if no one came to the auction?

"Someday," she thought, "someone will X-ray some young turk's art and find hints of ancient oils, mountain ranges overlain with blue watery color."

"Boring."

V was even more critical of herself, especially when she woke up alone and in pain, than she was of Conrad and his demise. V and Conrad, when he was alive, had had fun imagining what might be slopped over those old paintings

"Maybe the critics will imagine those ancient lines are a lost masterpiece!" This time she spoke out loud.

Once Caddie had caught her talking to the absent Conrad. After that, Caddie watched her more closely, with a knowing eye. Caddie, poor dear, already thought herself as old. She was in her early 70s. To have her ancient mother talk to her dead husband was a sign she (Caddie) was OK but what if when she got old….

"Caddie won't talk to me after I die," she had told the reappearing Conrad. "Although she hears my voice in her head, she says, especially when she forgets to brush her teeth."

V looked back at *The Times* photo again. "Pretty little photo," she said in her favorite snarky voice. "Really good for the travel business." It was what she called "false lying nostalgia," yearning for something that didn't exist. V had always tried to paint reality, to capture the sensations of awe that real landscape, with real terrors, presented to her. It was – and she sighed a very loud sigh – difficult.

"Conrad, do you remember that day at the Red Barn in Nevada? In the Amargosa Valley?"

II

V remembered it well – it was the day she saw what she had been looking at.

V was in the middle of her Red Barn art residency, 15 years before, in Nevada's Amargosa Valley. She had spent the day detailing and deepening her mostly finished canvases, seven of them, depicting the desert valley and mountains that ranged south from the Barn. It was 3:30; Conrad was on his way to drive her back to town. Having cleaned the brushes, she was leaning against the central post of the open barn doors. The desert floor and the Grapevine Mountains to the right filled her view close to the barn. The Funeral range, less vivid, spread on beyond the Grapevines where the sky widened and intensified. And, unseen but always in her consciousness, over the mountains, sunk flat into the desert, was Death Valley.

The mountains, without trees and grass, showed their rocks in falls of gray mats interrupted by colored bands of limestone. Broken rock, flowing like water, fanned from their bases, mixing iron oxide colors with lamp blacks. The ridges were folded into angular ravines that cut the folded and flat surfaces, making deep, mars black shadows. Lit by the sun, the ranges could shine a chromatic black, or perylene violet and olive, or indigo and burnt sienna. Sometimes V saw gold ochre with touches of Naples yellow. She imagined she could see sparkling quartz bits, even at the ten-mile distance. A primordial scene, always changing, always fascinating, ever challenging to paint.

The nearby Grapevines dominated the first three of her seven 4x8 foot canvases. She had used heavy globs of lamp and ivory blacks and deep umbers mixed with red oxides to sculpt and gouge and shadow the features. These nearer mountains were forceful, looming, pushing off the top of the canvases. The distant mountains, the Funerals, were smaller and narrower. They provided perspective and were smoother, more muted in color and shape. On the canvases depicting the far end of the range, the sky took over, cerulean blue fading into ultramarine, darkening at the top, taking up two thirds of the canvas. All the canvases' skies had transparency and infinitude; the mountains density and hardness. It was a beautiful monstrosity of a view.

As she rested against the Barn's door frame, V stared at the one, central set of shapes and rock that she had yet to capture on the panorama. Those ranges formed the transition between the Grapevines and the Funerals. And they refused to come into focus. V could not make out the ranges basic shapes, their indentations, shadows and highlights, the rock faces and crevices. The folds and color changes were there but fuzzy and undefined. She had tried at 9 am and 4 pm and noon, but neither the sky nor the sun would light up that middle section.

Until the moment – later she spoke of it as 3:37 p.m. – when the light arched over and laid wide open the crevices and crags of the central, transitional section of mountains. It came without warning. The clarity of the crevasses and sharp slopes made her gasp.

V grabbed her camera but failed, like *the Times* photographer, to make the camera's cyclops eye see what she saw. She swore out loud and thought – and this was the thought that became the catch phrase in the oft-told tale – "If only I were a painter, I would catch that -- in this light…."

And then – and only then --she realized she was a painter. The residency board had declared her to be one. She turned and pulled open her easel, grabbed her palette, and painted the center canvas of the 28-foot panorama. Although she had another three weeks at the Red Barn, she never again saw the central range in all its clarity.

III

A few years later V was asked to get an exhibit ready for a large space. She had new ideas for big paintings. She needed big canvases. So she sanded down and painted over most of the Amargosa Valley's 4x8-foot canvases. Later she wondered if she had scratched out the central panel, where the mountain had revealed itself. It was the moment when the whole scene became locked in paint, locked in her brain, locked in her heart. When she told Conrad that she painted over the Amargosa, he had said "That's probably OK. It wasn't one of your best."

He was right. Of course, he was. The newer paintings were better, more mature. Re-using the canvases was virtuous.

But she still thought about them. She had produced a large and pretty panorama, good enough paintings, so some said. The effort was there. The mountains were identifiable. But any depiction of that soaring lift she had felt at that vision, the moment when her breath caught and time seemed stopped -- that was not rendered.

IV

Thoughts about painted-over failures reminded her of last night's decision:

"Conrad, guess what! Today I'm leaving The Palouse at the Little Free Library."

V's spirits rose. She loved making decisions, and this was one that she had been obsessing over and discussing with Conrad for years.

The Palouse was a small painting, just 12 x 16 inches. It had been started and almost finished in one short stint on a snowfield in Washington State in mid-February. She and Conrad were driving home from another art residency, this one in Montana. They waited out a blizzard in a motel in Missoula and were impatient to be on the road and get back to Portland. When the skies and highways cleared, they traveled the snow-walled Interstate 90 through the Bitterroot Range, past Spokane and onto the glittering stretches of the eastern Washington State plateau. A cut-off road put them on a nicely plowed highway heading south to the Columbia River where they could pick up I-84 to Portland.

The highway crossed The Palouse.

The Palouse is eastern Washington's rolling plain, looking in its snowy state much like icy dunes. It stretched on all sides of the highway. V was gobsmacked by the enormous, mounded landscape. It surrounded their car, blue-white, purple, and glittering. It finished at a ridge of mountains on the far side of the distant Columbia River.

Driving the two-lane road, they passed a whitened gravel track that turned perpendicular to their roadway and also headed toward the mountains. The farm road was untouched by car tracks, glowing in the sun.

"Stop," V had said, sharply, to Conrad, who looked over at her and then slowed and stopped. "Back up," she said. "Turn down that lane."

He looked over at her again, and she waved her hand impatiently. The paved road was deserted; no cars had passed in either direction for the last half hour. He backed up, drove onto the snow-laden gravel cut, and then stopped in the middle of it.

V jumped out and pulled her painting equipment from the trunk. She stuck her collapsible easel into the untouched snow, put her plastic container of paints on the easel's support shelf, along with her brushes, and planted her painting stool through to gravel. The temperature was 10 degrees but the sun was pleasant, bright to the southwest. She put on her fingerless painting gloves.

Conrad sat in the car, heater running, listening to the All Classical station out of Portland. V made fast sketches of the whites of the snow. She added lavender and purple shadows where the fields fell into swales, and the distant black and blue-green ridge, which she knew was covered with ponderosas and cedars.

The road, a faint track through white waves and dried stalks of gold straw, was a tiny line through the enormity. The sky was bigger than the plains. The light was numinous. She was immersed in space and enthralled.

She painted for 20 minutes, until she couldn't feel her feet anymore. She packed the wet painting away into its box, stashed the rest of the equipment in newspaper, and climbed back into the car with Conrad.

"Whew!" she said. "Got it."

Conrad smiled and handed her a thermos of warm coffee.

"Lucky no truck-driving cowboy wanted to use the road," he said, as he backed onto the paved highway and started off.

V had a sudden spurt of guilt. "I never thought of that," she said. "I couldn't resist. Thank you for stopping."

Conrad wrinkled his nose at her and said, "It was a good break from driving."

And that was The Palouse. Or almost. After she got home, her mentor, a painter whose advice was quite sound, recommended that she add a touch of transparent yellow behind the far hills, giving a sense of a setting sun. She did so, with misgivings, but then, she already had misgivings about the painting. She hoped his suggestion, moving the eye across the scene, would change her doubts.

The touch of golden yellow did finalize the scene. It was conventionally satisfying -- but V was unhappy with it. What she had managed to capture and revise was a poor facsimile of her vision, not much more than a memory aid.

"You had to have been there," Conrad said.

V never exhibited The Palouse. She framed it, hoping formality would bring it to life. And then she stored it away. She refused to sell it to friends because she was afraid she'd see it when she visited them. She felt selling it to strangers would violate her standards. And so it sat, for fifteen or more years, taking up space on the attic shelves, taunting her, daring her to take it down and try to fix it.

It was unfixable because it was finished. The Palouse had the conventional layout, a road that pulled the eye across the scene to the distant glowing sky. It was perfectly executed, rich monochromatic hues with a balance and harmony that was like, well, like the three chord harmony of a Methodist church hymn. Satisfying, like mashed potatoes with a blob of margarine in the center.

And that was the problem, of course. None of those satisfactions were what caused V to order Conrad to stop the car in the middle of a snow-packed farm lane. The scene caught your breath, froze your heart. The painting was merely pretty.

V

V tucked the framed Palouse canvas into a grocery bag.

She put on her spring coat and old-lady walking shoes, and left the house, checking twice to make sure she had locked the door.

V no longer could walk further than a couple of blocks. But she still made new memories during those blocks, although without Conrad to hear her stories, the memories often vanished into the muddle of the day.

As she passed a modest house three doors down, she saw the kids who lived there digging into the soil under the lilac bush. They were gregarious youngsters who discussed with her the games they were playing. Once the five-year-old had whispered in a stage voice that Ms. V had a funny looking face but she really wished she could touch her hair to see if it was prickly. V had bent down and swished her hair toward the little girl. The child came running over and grabbed a swatch of V's long silver hair and fingered it. "It's so soft" she said. And won V's heart forever.

But today they were intent on digging. The 10-year-old looked up and said with the authority of the oldest child: "We are burying a gold finch that flew into our window this morning."

The little one said, "It's a pretty bird, but it's dead and we have to put it into the ground. Mama said under the lilac would be a good place. But we need to wrap it in something."

The older one looked annoyed. "I wanted to use a paper towel, but Daisy said that that would be too scratchy and would fall apart when it got wet. So then I said we should use her dolly blanket and that made her cry! She is such a crybaby – I had to call her out."

The ten-year-old sighed at her burden.

Daisy teared up again. "Dolly loves her soft blanket – see?" And she held up a piece of flannel, smeared with long ago faded colors and ground in grubby dirt.

V stood for a moment and then reached into her pocket. "I have a handkerchief that might work." It was a worn cotton rectangle that her grandmother had embroidered with yellow and purple pansies.

"Oh," said the ten-year-old. "That would be really nice."

"Oh oh," said the five-year-old. "Let me. It feels so soft. I want it. I want that for Dolly. Here, we can use the old blanket for the bird."

And so V watched the two children squabble over which was more important – for the bird to be honored with the pansies or for Dolly to have a new clean wrap. She finally handed over the handkerchief to Daisy and waved her hand in dismissal. The older child had height and age but Daisy had the object. Let them figure it out. The older child remembered her manners: "Thank you. Have a good day."

And V thought, oh yes, a lovely day. Here it is. I have a mission.

Down the block and around the corner, on a street arched by leafy green branches, there was a Little Free Library, housed in an old pie cabinet, painted pink, with French doors that opened onto four shelves of books donated by friends and neighbors. Beside the Library was a bowl of water for dogs and squirrels and cats and birds; the yard behind it was bushy, fully packed with spirea and beauty bush and thorny roses and bumptious hydrangeas.

V set the bag she was carrying down on the sidewalk and extracted the framed painting. She placed it against the cabinet behind the doggie bowl with a tag that said "Free." A note on the back gave the title, the date, the circumstances (10 degrees, snow, February, painted on-site) but nothing identified the artist.

And then she continued around the block, meeting only a dog walker who was talking on her phone and didn't glance up. V felt a sense of emptiness – a relief – the failure was out of her hands now – but also a betrayal --she was foisting an inferior product on an unsuspecting public, a painting she felt wasn't good. She was giving her failure to someone else. It was time to get rid of it, the painting and its reminder of failings. And yet, she was uneasy.

VI

Later, on her second walk of the day, V went back around the block. The children were gone but she saw the mound where the bird was laid to rest. She wanted to check on The Palouse. She had put out paintings with "Free" signs on them before, but they were ones she liked. The paintings that failed she gave away to young painters who sanded them down. But this day she put out a failed success; a painting other people liked and that she knew wasn't up to snuff. She decided as she walked that she would take the painting back. The young cartoonist who lived down the street loved making brightly colored shapes of comical animals over her sanded-over landscapes. He was always happy to receive her leftovers, and she liked looking at what he did.

Because a couple of people were standing by the Little Free Library, V walked on the other side of the street. As she came opposite the cabinet of books, she saw the young couple were holding the painting. The street was narrow; she could hear what they were saying. They were looking at the front and the back, and then the front again, passing it back and forth between them.

"It says 'Free'" said the young, roundish woman. She couldn't have been more than 18 and was cheaply dressed, with hair that needed cut.

"Yeah, it must be free and for anyone – there's no ID in the writing or anywhere." The guy had greasy hair and a pleasant tone of voice. V liked to hear people talk; tone as well as words enlarged their personalities.

"Should we take it? I mean, maybe it's only for people who live in this block? Or who like to read – it says, 'Library.'"

"I dunno. I don't see anyone else around. And the sign on it says 'Free.'" The guy touched his girl on the shoulder. "You really like it?"

"I love it. I really love it. The snow is all those colors but it's just white but all those colors – that's it," she said, touching the painting gingerly, as if the white would come off on her fingers.

"That's true," he said. "The snow out there is like that." He looked into the distant dark mountains, remembering: "We'll have to go out there next year when it snows. I mean, that blue and purple snow, I mean, just sorta blue, sorta purple just like it is. It was like that when I rode fence." He knew The Palouse

"And look at the sun up there behind the mountains – I mean it isn't a sun, just that we know the sun is there, behind the mountains. You know it's there, just going down. Would you take me there? I've never been." The young woman's voice was wistful.

"I seen that lots of times. It's really cold up there on the plateau. I wonder if the guy painted it in the cold. That would have been something."

The girl noticed V's presence across the street and looked at her in alarm. V walked a little faster, as if absorbed and not noticing. And when she turned the corner to go back home, she saw that the young guy was handing The Palouse to the woman who had gotten into the car. He glanced around but didn't see her. They smiled, big smiles, at one another, and he climbed into the Toyota and drove off. V felt something inside herself lurch.

She remembered a painting in the old rickety house where her parents had lived. "Whatever happened to that painting?" she wondered. She hadn't thought about it, perhaps had never really thought about it, although, because she could remember it, she must have looked at it a lot. But her nephew, when she inquired, said he couldn't find it when they cleaned up the old place.

It had hung, ever on the same wall, against the cluttered brown and yellow wallpaper of the kitchen, next to the bulletin board laden with photos of children and grandchildren and postcards she sent home from college. It was there, she was sure, in 2012, when she returned for her niece's wedding.

The ornately framed oil painting was either Victorian or neo-Victorian – not a great period for still lifes. It showed bulbous, heavy flowers in a round bottomed vase, some petals on a tabletop, clothed in a white tinted cloth. One fat rose lay, thorns and all, at the front bottom third of the painting. It was dark, overlain by years of greasy dust. The other things hanging on the wall, besides the photos of children long grown, were five-and-dime images on velvet, "oriental" scenes drawn with straw, flower prints, and big-eyed children images cut from magazines taped to the wallpaper. Nothing on the walls of that kitchen was hung with any thought as to where other things were – if there was a space and someone liked something and there was a nail available, it was hung up. And forgotten.

And yet, in her mind, the oil painting, an original, was there. And she was there, a five and six and seven-year-old, watching the family and friends and ashtrays and coffee cups and noticing the painting which was different from the magazine prints of poppies and daisies. It was mysterious, it called to be touched and investigated, although she never knew what she was investigating.

But now, the painting had disappeared. The house was a summer gathering place for various nieces and nephews, the photos on the bulletin board faded, and the wallpaper still intact. But the painting was gone, thrown away or hidden in an attic somewhere.

And here she was, 3,000 miles away, having disappeared a different painting, one with a history that no one would know. The painting would reappear in a cheap apartment somewhere and become a shared story for the young couple, who might or might not stay together, who might or might not remember their awe at the colors that snow holds, but who might keep hold of that twinge of the awe that she had felt.

It was enough. She went home and told Conrad, and he smiled and said that he knew that that would happen someday. And then she looked at his empty chair, shook her head, and sat down.

DECORUM

Monday

I figured when I first saw her that she had been a natural redhead. And then, when her hair went salt-and-pepper, she became a *dedicated* redhead. But now the hair was red only at the tips, the rest having grown out in a drab yellow-silver-brown limpness. It had been cut, most likely with kitchen scissors.

She came limping up the café ramp from the antique store at a snail's pace and clutched the railing along the sloped surface. Each movement she made deepened the hollows along her eyes and mouth.

I know that walk. Her hips were grinding like mine did before I got them replaced. Ralph, who had set down across the table from me, was busy with his tuna fish sandwich and didn't notice the sorry-lookin' woman making her way up the ramp. Ralph is a guy and doesn't ever notice much. Today he had a fat book with diagrams and stuff and barely said hello when he sat down at my table.

When the former redhead reached the top of the ramp, she stopped and studied the café, and I knew she was a newbie at Monti's. She sat down at the first table beside the ramp, a big one. She had on wrinkled blue jeans and a faded cardigan sweater with a flared bottom that bunched above her hips. The sweater, a musty brown, was badly pilled.

When she sat down, her face fell into a soft rectangle, with deep wrinkles outlining her nose and mouth. The shape comes to us round-faced cuties when we age. and gravity pulls our chubby cheeks into old lady jowls. I'm shocked when I catch a glimpse of myself in the mirror.

The woman looked toward the counter where various staff members worked. No one looked back at her. At Monti's Café you go to the cash register, tell them what you want, pay for it, get your own coffee, and somebody brings you your food. Today I was having an avocado bagel, a cookie, and thinking about a mimosa. Spouse Jake was at home fixing the car, and Elizabeth, my daughter, was in town for a while but had to work. So she was in our spare bedroom, thumping away at her laptop, and I was having lunch by myself at Monti's. By myself because Ralph is no company at all.

The kinda-redhead, in her 70s, sat for a while and then got up and got herself a glass of water. She watched the ordering line at the counter. Then she looked over at Ralph and me.

"Looks like a good sandwich." She spoke clearly and without a smile.

"It is," I said.

"You order at the counter, and they bring it to you." Ralph didn't look up from his book but he knew the question.

The woman looked down the ramp, then made her way across the room to the counter. Bridget Clare, long-time Monti's server, took her through the posted menu and accepted her order and cash. The woman dropped a couple of dollars into the tip jar and made her way back to her seat. Bridget Clare brought her coffee.

No one at Monti's ever brings me my coffee, although the manager, Glenda, sometimes brings a mimosa so she can catch up on the gossip.

The redhead had barely taken a bite of her bagel and cream cheese when a small child came up the ramp, looking around cautiously. The little girl spotted the woman through the ramp's railings and jumped a little, with a big smile.

"Grandma!" she shouted, and peered up through the posts.

"Oh Mellykin, hi. Where's Barbara? You were supposed to stay with her."

Grandma wagged her fingers over the railing. The little girl came into the café dining area and plunked down on a chair across from her grandmother. She was dressed in a pink skirt and red top and had on yellow and green checked tights. Her legs dangled over the edge of the chair seat.

"Babs is hanging around books, reading. She wouldn't even come and look at the pet rock I found." Mellykin's voice was high and loud. "It was really awesome – had googly eyes that went all around it. They go around and around when you shake it. And it looked pretty, um, pretty, well, I think I want to get it."

Grandma sat up a bit and her lips moved up at the corners.

"A pet rock? Oh well, Amelia, I bet you can afford it." Grandma paused. "But will you take care of it? That's always the question with a pet, you know." Grandma looked at the child intently.

Amelia-Mellykin looked puzzled. "How do you take care of a rock?" She hadn't considered this problem.

"Well, let's see," said Grandma. "I don't imagine rocks eat much, do you? Although your rock might be different."

"Can I really get it? What do I do? Come back into the store and get it for me." Amelia squirmed around the hard seat. "I'm sure I can take care of it, I'm sure."

Grandma nodded. "We'll get it when the others have decided on their purchases," she said.

"But what if it goes away while I'm up here?"

Amelia moved to the edge of the seat, putting her feet on the floor.

"Rocks are like slugs – very very slow," said Grandma, putting on a thinking face. "In fact, I think they are much slower than slugs. I've seen some in the desert that can move a foot or so in a month, but that's really fast for a rock."

"What desert? Was it where you went when grandpoppa died? Where you flew to?" Amelia's voice was high-pitched.

Grandma said, quiet enough I had to strain to hear: "Yes. It's called Death Valley and it has rocks that slide across the sand. I'll show you photos when we get home."

"Amelia, what are you doing up there? I've been looking all over for you." A loud voice shouted up the ramp. Amelia went to the railing and looked down.

"I'm up here with Grandma." She yelled. "You weren't talking to me, reading that dumb book. And I needed to find out if my – my purchase" she paused to make sure "purchase" was the right word, "if my special purchase was OK."

A teenager came up the ramp, her Doc Martens thumping hollowly. She looked angry and relieved -- and then self-conscious.

Other customers, alerted by the yelling, were looking at her. She slowed down and came to sit beside her grandmother. She had Jello red hair with blue streaks, ringlets plastered with greasy cream.

"I couldn't find her," she explained to her grandmother. "I was just looking at a book, and when I looked up, she wasn't there."

"It's OK, sweetie, no harm." Grandma nodded. "Amelia knew where to find me. Where are the guys, do you know?"

I looked at Ralph. He looked at me. Two children and one grandmother are a lot. More children are a lot more.

"They're OK, just looking at kid's stuff. I couldn't find anything I wanted for $5, Grandma." The teenager tried on a whiny voice. "Can I have an advance?"

"Now Barbara, you know the rules. Five dollars a day for each day of this week. You can spend it all at once at the end or…"

"Dumb rules," Barbara mumbled.

"Dumb or not, that's what we agreed when we came here. And you can have anything you want to eat. I'm paying."

Grandma used a very patient voice. She could have patented it.

"I'm not hungry," said Barbara. "And where are the guys, anyway? Can we go back to your house now?"

Grandma, not smiling, shook her head. Her face, with its mapped ridges and valleys and fallen hills, was stern, like you'd see in an old-fashioned photograph. And up the ramp came a couple of boys, one looking to be about 8 and the other a couple years older. Both had baggy pants and T-shirts featuring superhero characters. They bounced into the empty chairs, squirming and kicking the table legs.

"Grandma, Grandma, we found a Slinky." The younger boy had a high-pitched voice like his sister, although he wasn't quite so loud. "I remember you used to have a Slinky at your house. It would go down the stairs. It was awesome. And this one is only six dollars and fifty cents."

I was horrified. Six-fifty for an old toy. Ralph looked at me and grinned. I remembered a Slinky I got for my girls a long time ago. It got mangled and tangled too fast but they had fun with it while it lasted.

"There was some information on the box, Grandma, and it's really old, I mean the original Slinky. This one is newer." The older boy's voice broke a little.

"It's shiny so we think it's new," the younger boy added.

"The booklet inside the box said that it makes a sound that changes when you swing it around or something. What happened to the Slinky you used to have?"

"You read the instructions? Oh Gene," Grandma's eyebrows raised as she pinned the older boy with a glance. "I hope you didn't open the box. Bennie, would you sit still, please?"

"But what happened to that old Slinky?" Bennie asked, kicking the table leg again. "If you still have it we won't have to spend our money."

"Oh dear, I think I threw it out after Grandpoppa died." The boys stilled themselves, resting their hands on arms of the chairs. It was quiet for a minute.

"Well, then I want to buy it to see if the booklet is right." Gene said.

"No, I want to buy it." Bennie wheeled around to his brother. "I saw it first." And suddenly the table was in a clamor, the older girl telling the younger ones to quiet down, the boys arguing, Amelia saying she wanted her pet rock, and Grandma trying to hush them.

The rest of us at Monti's listened; some of us were amused.

"Sure glad that isn't my bunch," said Ralph, leaning close to my ear. "That's a handful."

At some point, Grandma, whose lowered eyebrows were inching toward one another, told Barbara to take the children to the counter to decide which cookie each wanted.

As the kids went up to the counter, Grandma looked over at us and shook her head.

"It's the teachers' strike," she said. "The kids have to go somewhere. And I was elected as the 'where'." Her eyes lightened a little and the brows widened. We smiled at her.

"So every day we're coming to Monti's after lunch. Then we'll go home and have a rest – I will rest and they'll argue – and then their Dad will pick them up after he's through work. The cookie should hold them until he comes. Although what he'll feed them, I don't know. Their Mom tends to work late – she's my youngest – anyway, they're good kids. Just a little noisy, that's all. Hope we aren't bothering you folks too much."

And back they trooped, cookies in hand, shredding crumbs and chatter. And once they had finished eating and slurped the last of their drinks, they went back down the ramp, Grandma limping behind them, to check out pet rocks and new Slinkys. Ralph and I sat back with coffee (him) and mimosa (me) and thought about trying to handle four kids for five or six hours.

And were relieved we didn't have to. And glad for the family that they had Grandma.

Tuesday

The next day, I left Jake and daughter Elizabeth discussing afternoon chores. I avoided Jake's tofu lunch and was having a bacon and avocado bagel. While I was eating, Grandma came slowly up the ramp.

"Who got the Slinky, Bennie or Gene?" I asked, after she had ordered and sat down.

Bridget Clare brought her her coffee.

"Undecided," sighed Grandma. "But today," she straightened up a bit, "they get $5 more to spend, so if there are two Slinkys, they can each have one. We were tired out yesterday from the excitement," the corners of her mouth went up just a tiny bit, "so we got the pet rock and Amelia got the change, and we went home, and I fell in a heap on the couch. Now I'm having a battle with Barbara about tattoos." She rolled her eyes and her eye brows followed.

She took a bite of her cream cheese bagel.

"Argh, tattoos – that sounds like a bother." I don't like tattoos on lovely young skin, male or female.

"They're illegal in Portland for anyone under 18 – she's 16 – but she's obsessed and there's a tattoo parlor –uh, salon – just down the street. I'm not going to let her go window shopping, but that means a battle. Maybe something downstairs will catch her eye."

She got in two more bites of her bagel before Barbara came stomping up the steps.

"Amelia's mooning over some little china animals. She knows where to find me. And I don't know where the guys are, last time I saw them they were fighting over a tin whistle, blowing it so the whole store was in agony. I was so embarrassed!" Barbara sat down in one of the hard chairs.

"Want a cookie?" Grandma asked.

"No. It's fattening -- sugar and lard and stuff. People who eat cookies die."

True, I thought, but there was more to it than that. I didn't say anything. Grandma took another bite of her bagel.

"I'm getting a diet Coke." Barbara announced. Grandma handed her some money and she marched to the counter, not looking at anyone.

"Whew!" I said. Grandma nodded. She looked grim.

Across the café, at the far end, a boy, perhaps 15, was eyeing Barbara. I gestured with the back of my hand and rolled my eyes toward him. Grandma looked over.

"Well, maybe that's a distraction," she murmured. Barbara came back, sat down, and put her Coke on the table.

"Change please," said Grandma. Barbara dumped the change on the table.

"Did you tip?" Grandma asked.

"Do I have to? They didn't do anything."

"Oh Barbara, yes, you know the drill. Go put the change in the tip jar."

Barbara got up and caught a glimpse of the boy across the room. She looked away quickly but not before Grandma and I both noticed.

"We discussed tipping before we left home, but she's stubborn. It's been hard – she adored her grandfather and after he died, she couldn't quite get her old self back. But she was showing signs of becoming human again. We all have hope…."

Barbara was back.

"So, did you find anything you liked today?"

"Just a couple of pair of earrings, but they were too expensive, not like kids' toys, they want real money -- $15 -- $20 for a tiny pair." Barbara's grievances' spilled over.

"I should get more money," she said, "I'm the oldest, and besides I'm supposed to be babysitting the kids, so I deserve more."

Grandma looked at her and shook her head. "True, you are the oldest kid, but I'm the oldest grandma. And we all agreed to the rules. Montabella is a big store, with lots of stuff, and by Friday you'll have seen everything and can make a thoughtful choice. Now be a good kid and go find out what Amelia is doing."

Barbara got up, breathed a loud sigh, and then, after looking at the male teenager across the room, went down the ramp. A few minutes later he followed her.

Amelia came skipping back up the ramp.

"Grandma, Grandma, I found a couple more pet rocks. And there's a book about how to take care of them. They're really cute – one has a bow and another has these big teeth that are really really ugly."

Grandma stopped frowning and nodded to Amelia. "So, are you going to get another one?"

"I don't know. There are too many choices. Come down and see them. They are really cute. The book is expensive – four dollars and seventy-five cents. But I can maybe read it quick in the store and follow the instructions without buying it. Like Barbara standing in the aisles, reading her old book. But now she's by the earrings, talking to a guy."

Amelia was the town crier.

"What are the boys doing?"

"Oh I dunno. They saw one of those cube things that you turn around and around and then they saw a wind-up sort of thing with a motorcycle but Gene said it was too much money, like $20, but Bennie tried it out on the floor until the guy came along and told him not to mess with it unless he were going to buy it. And Gene said the rider was a girl and he wasn't interested in any old girl toy, so they went off down another aisle and I found the other pet rocks. I wonder if there are any more in the store."

Amelia whirled back and forth on her chair as she chatted. Grandma looked as if her hip was hurting.

"Want a cookie?" she asked Amelia.

Amelia stopped and nodded, and Grandma held out some bills for her.

"Can I get it all by myself?" Amelia's eyes went wide.

"Just bring me back the money that's left over," said Grandma. We watched to see if Monti's staff could deal. Amelia went up to the counter and stood on her tiptoes, shouting to make herself heard. Then she ran back to Grandma and said "She wants to know if I want anything to drink."

"Of course you do. Get some lemonade, like yesterday." Grandma shooed her back to the cash register, where Bridget Clare patiently waited.

"They grow up fast," said Grandma. I nodded, although it was unlikely I was going to see this crowd growing. They would remain for me as they were, 6, 9, 12, and 16, girl, boy, boy, girl, and Grandma, containing the chaos, just barely. Sometimes I think that that makes my Monti encounters perfect. I don't have to know about the ever-afters.

When Amelia brought her lemonade back to the table, Grandma stood up and took her over to the tip jar, whispering in her ear. Amelia carefully counted out some coins and dropped them in the jar. She beamed at her grandma, who nodded solemnly back.

Wednesday

Wednesday I arrived at Monti's a little late – Elizabeth and I had weeded for a while, and I had asked her about planting a garden. When I suggested going to Monti's (I wanted to see if Grandma and kids were there) she begged off. Her work report is due right after she flies back east. So I was late and hungry and alone.

Grandma was in her seat, with an egg and bacon bagel. I ordered one for myself at the counter and took it to the table next to Grandma. Ralph has already taken his usual seat; he gestured at the other side of the table, so I sat down.

"How's the day so far?" I asked. "Decision time for the shoppers?"

Grandma looked over at us. "It's $15 today and they are in a twitch. Too much money, not enough money. They're bored and tired of my house and my lunches and want to call their friends on my phone -- their dad took theirs away from them last week when they refused to help him out with the laundry. They think I should share my phone -- I didn't fall for that. And thank God it's Wednesday. Only two more days." She shook her head as her wrinkles deepened. "At least, only two more days unless there's more. News on the strike doesn't sound good."

I nodded my head and looked sympathetic. I was sympathetic.

"So what are they thinking of buying today?"

"Barbara isn't saying – she isn't saying anything at all, in fact. She's decided talking is old guy stuff. And Gene was looking at a complicated Rubik's Cube, letting Bennie have the Slinky. And then he, Gene, discovered a whole shelf of used science fiction books, so he's settled in a bit. Bennie, though, isn't fond of reading and keeps nagging Gene to come see the hand carved fire engine he found – much too expensive, of course – and the cardboard puzzles, which I keep telling him probably have missing pieces."

"What's Amelia up to?"

"Oh Amelia, she's good for everything. She's moved on from pet rocks, although she goes back to check up on them once in a while. Yesterday it was tiny tea sets and little cat figurines and today I haven't heard yet, but Barbara said she had found a doll scarf for Amelia's favorite stuffed toy."

I thought about that for a moment. "It's nice that Barbara is helping out with the others – must take a bit off your shoulders."

"It does," said Grandma, "Although she puts her own stuff on me. Yesterday she sulked all day because the ring she found was too expensive -- $27 – and the guy she had met had to leave early because his dad was picking him up. And when I asked her to pick up the towels from the bathroom floor, she slammed the door on me. Ah well, it's only a few days until the weekend."

"How is the strike going?"

The teachers' strike was awkward. Jake and I were all for the teachers, but here she was, four kids on her hands and who knows what she thought about unions and stuff.

"I only know what I read in the paper – and" she did that little quirk at the edge of her lips that I decided was a smile, "I haven't had much time to read the paper lately. But their dad says the teachers are making good points, so there's that. And my neighbor says that everyone sympathizes with the teachers – buying their own supplies and helping the poorer kids with breakfasts and lunches during the strike. So it's not bad yet. Of course, there's no school. And there's Barbara…."

Grandma's voice trailed off, just as Barbara came up the ramp. Barbara's hair was newly jelled in lime green. Grandma's hair was limper than it had been on Monday. "Grandma!" Barbara spoke over the railing in a low urgent voice.

"Grandma, can I go for a walk? Just down the street – there's that yarn shop and fabric dyeing place…"

"And the tattoo parlor," interrupted Grandma. "And are you going alone?"

Barbara raised her chin a bit.

"James said he could use a little air," she said, pronouncing "James" with precision.

"And who is James?" Grandma knew precisely who James was, as he had been following Barbara around for hours, but she needed to play the role of chaperone.

I wondered if kids had chaperones these days. Maybe at school dances – just a little extra job for the teachers' boring Friday nights.

"James lives down on 89th – he's out of school too. We both have been inside a lot this week – and you know it isn't healthy to be inside all the time. We need fresh air. Please, Grandma," and her voice stopped being stiff. "Pretty please – he's only in tenth grade, but he knows some of my friends and I'm so so bored, please Grandma, we'll just walk around the block."

Grandma thought for a moment, mostly, I thought, to make sure Barbara knew it was a tough decision. "OK, but no more than 20 minutes. After that I call the cops. And bring James back here and I'll buy him a bagel or something."

Barbara turned and bounced on the ramp and then straightened up to finish her walk with dignity. James greeted her. Grandma looked at me and shook her head. Then she leaned over the railing and said, in a clear loud voice: "And stay away from the tattoo parlor." The two kids scurried out of sight. She sat back, shaking her head.

Thursday

Thursday Jake dropped me off at Monti's (he had to get a blood draw from the medical lab across town). Elizabeth was in a Zoom call when we left. I thought I might have to get two mimosas.

Grandma was already established at her table. I sat down at the table next to it, facing her.

"Jake's gone for a lab draw," I said, as if she had asked.

"Nothing wrong, I hope." She added, "Of course, lab tests will find something wrong, even if there isn't."

I grinned at her. "Ain't it the truth?" Then I looked around. "No kids around to hear me say 'ain't', I hope."

This time the edges of her eyes as well as her lips turned up. "I think they've heard a bit worse here and there," she said.

"So what are they looking at today?"

Grandma's face fell. "Well, Barbara's looking at the young man's face, I suspect, although there aren't many places in the store where canoodling can go on. I don't know what the limits are among teens these days – I'm just hoping to make it through Friday."

"How's the strike coming along?"

"Lordy, I don't know. One of the mothers at the Facebook site said she thought the negotiations were into the nitty-gritty, so there's that. But then someone else said the board was stuck on class size, and another person said that they were refusing to deal with broken windows and rodents and leaky roofs. It's all such a mess."

"It always is – strikes seem to air out all kinds of dirty laundry."

Grandma nodded. "Dirty laundry indeed. Do you know how many showers a 16-year-old can take in a day? Each one with a clean towel because her brothers have dried their hands on the last one she used. And no one picks up a towel from the floor unless I remind them. Which I do. Which gets tiresome." She shook her head. "Pray for the strike to be over, OK? Especially if you have any influence."

Her voice was stronger and ironic. Just the idea of the strike being over perked her up.

I shook my head. "No influence on heaven. And not on the school board, either. And here's Amelia."

Amelia was standing on the ramp, looking through the bottom of the railing at her grandma. When Grandma caught her eye, she bounced up the ramp like a pogo stick. The ramp shook. Grandma rolled her eyes and prepared her stern face for the six-year-old.

"I found something." Amelia's voice was high and loud, as usual. She bounced up the ramp and plopped on a chair. "Grandma, I found something. Look, see what I found."

She opened her fist and inside were plastic beads, some with the paint chipped off, in shades that ranged from mauve to light pink to very light yellow and puke green. Each bead had an extension on one side of it and a hole on the other.

"See," Amelia picked out two pinkish beads and pushed the extension of one into the hole of the other. "See, they fit together and you can use any color you want with any other and the next day put them together in a different way. I can make them match my shirt."

"Oh, that's really nice. How many beads did you get?

"See, that's the thing, they're priced by the bead, so each bead is 10 cents and the lady said I can get ten for one dollar. And then I have a bunch of money left over. Or, if I get eleven I will get dimes and quarters."

Amelia had discovered the joy of noisy money.

"So Grandma, I got you a bracelet."

Grandma's eyes widened. "Oh that's so nice, Amelia, but I think you should keep it for yourself. You found it and it's your money, you know."

"No no Grandma, I'll get lots more for myself to make a necklace. And maybe a bracelet for Barbara."

The sad beads, looking grubby in her hands, just about gave me a stomach ache. I remember pop beads. They were ugly when they were new, when I wanted beads that were transparent and made of glassy stones that felt cold and heavy on my wrist. These weren't worth 10 cents altogether.

"Thank you, darling," said Grandma. "Perhaps you can put the bracelet together for me."

Amelia, tongue clutched between her teeth, put together the bracelet and fastened it on her grandmother's arm. Grandma sent her to the counter with money for a cookie.

"Nice kid," I said.

"I hated those things when they were new and they don't improve with age," said Grandma. "I hope Barbara keeps her mouth shut when she sees them."

And, of course, immediately the two boys and Barbara came up the ramp, Bennie charging on ahead of Gene, Barbara walking self-consciously. I caught a glimpse of her suitor hanging out below.

"Ewww, what's that ugly thing on your wrist?" Barbara's taste was good, so there was that.

"Hush. Amelia got it for me. And she's getting one for you too, so be nice."

"Ugh."

"Be nice to Amelia – she's thinking of you, even if her taste is still, um, young."

All this had been watched by the two younger boys, who then proceeded to rat out their sister and her boyfriend who had done nothing but stand in a corner of the big store and talk and it was all so boring, even though Gene had found a nifty Magic 8-Ball that asked questions that even he had trouble answering. And, Bennie added, Barbara's boyfriend didn't know the answers and never even looked at them, just kept talking to Barbara, who pretended to be bored, but Gene could see that she was just pretending and was really excited.

"I bet they will do some kissy-face" said Bennie. Gene rolled his eyes. Grandma's voice was sharp.

"Go get yourself your cookie for the day, boys, before they get all gone."

The boys and Barbara left to argue over lemonade and Pepsi.

Grandma sat back with something that sounded like a groan. "One more day," she said. "One more day."

She looked at me. "I'm Esther, by the way."

"I'm Willy – Wilma Jean when I'm bad." Saying this sometimes made people smile.

Esther sighed and her long square face turned into a sharp-edged rectangle. "I had just gotten past the worst of grief over Fred's dying and thought I might get my hair done and go out with my friends and then the strike happened."

"Oh, that's hard. Um, how long…."

"Oh, it's been a year and two months. But we were close. And he did a lot of things that I forgot had to be done, and then I had to do all the money stuff and notifications and close out accounts. It could have been worse, I suppose, but it was hard. And he wasn't there."

"How are the children?"

"They're resilient, that's the truth of it. For which I'm glad. Barbara was hit hardest. She named her grandfather– she stuttered when she was little and added the extra "pa" to "Pop" and we all thought it was charming and made it sorta French and it stuck. 'Grand-pop-pa.' My husband liked that.

"I retired early to take care of him – that was good – but now I'm out of the loop. It's hard to find friends and company after you've isolated yourself for a couple of years."

Esther looked down at the table. Then she looked up and the tiredness receded from her eyes.

"I'm going to have dinner on Saturday with my best friend from high school – and I've made a hair appointment. She always goes shopping with me so I'm hoping for a trip to the mall. I changed sizes over the last year, so at least some new jeans and shirts and maybe a nice outfit for going out to dinner."

Small steps I thought. And I thought of Jake. He too does things all day that I've forgotten need doing. He's getting up in years and is slowing down and I try to do more, but when I do, I see all the more that he does. It's scary.

"It must be scary, taking on all the chores by yourself."

Esther nodded, her softening look disappearing. "It's OK. And I get to eat over the sink. And stay in bed in the morning without him looking in to see if I'm dead." She snorted lightly. "So there's that."

And suddenly the space was filled with the four children, carrying drinks and cookies and shoving at each other as they fussed about who got which chair and which chair was the best one.

And then, bam! It was crazy. Loud, banging confusion.

The kids' voices shot up in shouts and yells. Bennie said something nasty. Barbara looked over to see if I heard. Gene, who had been sitting closest to me, stretching and poking at the others, jumped up and smacked Bennie on the arm. Bennie pushed his brother with both hands, and before I knew what was happening, my mimosa was splattered everywhere and the glass broke into a million pieces. Cookies tumbled from the big table and one Pepsi can went spinning. Then Gene tumbled into my lap and his elbow went into my bad knee. I yelped and tried to stand up, but the squirming weight of boy on my lap pushed me back down.

Grandma was there before I figured out what to do. She pulled Gene off me, glared at both of us, shook the boy a little and then pushed him behind her.

"Are you OK?" she demanded.

"Uh, yes, sure, I think so. Splashed a little, but OK." I didn't want to admit that my knee hurt.

"I'll pay for dry cleaning," said Esther, looking at my LL Bean vest and jeans. She was grim, angry, stiff, and in control.

"You, Gene, outside! Benjamin – go join your brother." Esther's voice was not loud but really scary. "Out, out the main café door, not through the store! Barbara, go with them and hold them there until I clean up this mess."

Esther – Grandma – forgot her hurting hips and taking hold of the boys' shoulders, one on either side, marched them to the door.

"Out. And then wait for me."

Then she came back.

She looked at me and said again, "I'm sorry. I should have been watching them more closely." She didn't sound exactly sorry, more like the general, cleaning up after the troops.

"Amelia, go out with Barbara and don't move away from her."

She turned to Bridget Clare and Glenda, who had come out from behind the counter when the ruckus began. Bridget Clare handed me a clean towel to wipe off mimosa splashings. Glenda stood behind her, as straight and tall as Esther.

Esther faced Glenda. "I will pay for the broken glass and the extra work your staff has to do to clean up the mess," she said. "I must talk to the children first, but I will be back."

She strode outside, leaving the whole café silent and agog. I moved to another table and circled my knee around to see if it was really OK. Bridget Clare found a broom and mop and she and Glenda cleaned up the mess. Then Bridget Clare made me another mimosa.

"On the house," she said, sitting it down quietly. She shook her head at me, and joined Glenda behind the counter. The café was very subdued.

I admit I was shaking a little. It all went so fast and was so loud and confusing and then, when Esther took charge, it was over.

Grandma Esther and the children had gone across the street, to a little park that we could see through the front windows. She was sitting on a bench with her back to the café. The children were lined up in front of her. The whole Café watched as she addressed each child individually. Bennie was first and we could see him talking and then go quiet and start rubbing his eyes and face. I imagined snot and tears, all over his sleeve.

Gene was next up. He didn't look at his grandmother, but stared fixedly into the ground. Then he answered a question, but was interrupted, first by Bennie, who was silenced by Esther's hand, and then by Esther herself. Gene got more rigid. He seemed to be answering in monosyllables, but Esther didn't let up. Finally, she turned to Barbara who looked small and worried and kept her head down, lifting only her eyes; and then Amelia came in for her turn. She threw herself into her grandmother's lap. Esther put her back on her feet. Further talking on Esther's part.

Then there was a long group talk. Gene stood at the edge of the others, but listened, and nodded yes when directly addressed. Grandma finally nodded, got up from the bench slowly, and the group came back into the café.

Gene walked over to me, very slowly. He didn't look at me and talked fast.

"I'm sorry," he said, "if I hurt you. I will use my allowance to clean your clothes."

I started to dismiss his offer, but Grandma glared at me and I stopped.

Bennie came next and said to me, “It was my fault. I got mad when he pinched me and I forgot to control my temper which isn’t right and I pushed him too hard.”

He looked at Grandma and back at me. “I pushed him when I should have found another way to make him stop and I’m sorry, I’m really sorry, I hope you don’t hurt too bad and I’m going to put my allowance in with Gene’s so your clothes are OK and also the broken glass, although that was Gene’s fault, except” another quick look at Grandma, “it was really mine too.”

He stepped back behind his grandmother.

Barbara looked at the floor and talked so softly I had to lean forward to hear.

“I was supposed to be watching out for those two because sometimes they do act up and I know the signals but I, I wasn’t paying attention.”

She scraped the floor with her foot. “And so I am sorry too. I hope you aren’t hurting but if you are I can help you to your car or home or whatever. And I’m good at weeding dandelions. I should have been paying more attention.”

And finally Amelia, loud and clear: “I saw them starting to push and shove and then Gene pinched Bennie and I know Bennie hates to be pinched and I could have jumped over and stopped Bennie from shoving Gene – I think I could have.”

She looked at me and tilted her head. “Anyway, I am sorry you got hurt and the pretty glass got broken and you lost your drink and if I can help you stand up or anything, I will or anything else, maybe you would like a bracelet like Grandma’s.”

At that, Esther put her hand on Amelia's shoulder and stopped her. She nodded to me, I said something about being OK and that I accepted their sorries. Then she turned to Glenda and Bridget Clare, who were watching.

Esther made sure all the children were turned toward the two women.

"We are all sorry we made such a terrible scene in your nice restaurant. The children will pay for the damages and the extra work."

She turned to each child. Barbara held out her daily allowance, $5, and said, "I am very sorry. If we owe more, we'll come in tomorrow and pay." The other children followed suit, Gene having to fish out his tightly folded bill from his pocket. Glenda waited patiently. Finally he got it straightened out and handed it over.

Glenda looked at each of the kids. Their faces were mottled and reddish, some tear-stains remained. They all stood very still.

"Thank you," said Glenda. "I accept your apologies and the money will cover the damages." Then she went back behind the counter. "I figured that the total was more like $15."

She started to hand a five dollar bill back to Grandma. Grandma Esther shook her head.

"The extra is for making so much noise and mess in your nice restaurant." She lowered her voice. "And besides, I can't get into dividing up the remainder."

Glenda looked at her and then smiled.

"We'll not come back tomorrow, I promise," said Esther. "I won't put you through this again."

Bridget Clare stepped out from behind the counter. She spoke directly to the children.

"I think you need to come back tomorrow," she said. "You need to show us that you can be good customers."

She turned to Esther. "I hope you'll bring the family back in tomorrow." And then she smiled her big warm smile.

And added: "I just saw on my phone that the strike is ended, and school will start up again on Monday."

Esther, looking exhausted, nodded at Glenda, at Bridget Clare, at the assembled diners, and finally at me. The family silently left the café. They walked down the sidewalk past the windows, looking mostly straight ahead. Bennie had taken Amelia's hand and the two young ones walked in front. Gene was behind them, stiff in his gait, and Barbara, staring at the sidewalk, stayed at the back with her grandmother. Esther reached up and touched Barbara's shoulder and then withdrew her hand and limped along. They turned the corner and were out of sight.

Friday

My knee survived Gene's weight although I was gimpy on Friday. I came early to Monti's – Elizabeth was finishing up her report and Jake was hurrying through mowing the lawn because there was an important game coming up on the TV.

When I got there, the café was almost empty. After greeting Bridget Clare and announcing I was just fine, I ordered a chicken on croissant with salad. Neither Grandma nor the children were anywhere to be seen.

Suddenly the three younger children, followed by Barbara and her guy, came up the ramp and took over the table next to me. The older children, sitting quietly, looked at the counter, where Bridget Clare waved to them. Then they looked over at me. I smiled.

Amelia, irrepressible, bounced over to me and said, in her most triumphant voice: "We got Grandma an elephant. A big elephant! With a bow on its trunk and on its tail and you can see inside it where there are all kinds of colored lines that swirl around. Show her, Babs...."

Barbara brought out a bulky glass form from under her sweater.

She said, "I needed to hide it from Grandma, but they said someone would think I was shoplifting, so one of the check-out ladies walked us to the ramp."

Barbara relaxed then, just a little. "Then Grandma came down another aisle and told us that she was going to the bathroom and the checkout lady pretended she was not there and so here we are."

"Grandpoppa always said Grandma must be cooking for an elephant because she made so much food." Sai Amelia, turning back and forth.

Gene went up to the counter to get a brownie. He told Bridget Clare, with great precision, about the elephant -- "all glass, 'blown glass' is what it said on the label, but it's shaped like a real elephant with a big trunk that is hollow, just like it should be. Though it doesn't make any noise it looks just like an elephant, trumpeting."

Bridget Clare said it sounded like a great present. She and Glenda followed Gene back to the table, where Barbara showed them the bow-decorated, multi-colored, striped glass figure. It was impressively big. Bridget Clare went to the counter and found a candle to put in the elephant's upraised trunk. It fit perfectly.

"But it's not her birthday," said Gene.

"But it could be the birthday of the school re-opening," said Bridget Clare. "Are you excited about going back to school?"

"Grandma is," said Barbara, and all four kids giggled, Bennie holding his hand over his mouth. Barbara laid the candle on the table by the elephant.

The children went to the counter to order their treats. Barbara pulled out the money Grandma had given her. I imagined that Esther was having a time-out, locking herself in the store's bathroom.

"Is this enough money for our food? Grandma isn't here to pay." Barbara asked Bridget Clare. Barbara was nervous; the others were ordering Cokes and brownies, which cost twice as much as cookies and lemonade. "That's plenty," said Bridget Clare and gave her some change, which Barbara dropped into the tip jar. Barbara had ordered a biscotti and coffee.

"Did you give them a tip?" Amelia had been counting, loudly, the different kinds of bagels stacked alongside the cookie display.

"Of course, dummy. You always give them a tip – it's only fair."

Barbara took the black mug to the coffee stand. She stared at the labels and then put the cup under the French roast dispenser. She took a sip and made a face and added as much half-and-half as the cup would hold. She gulped down a mouthful and added more cream.

Back at the table Bennie was assigned to watch out for Grandma.

"Let's put the elephant on her chair."

"Which chair? Here, put my sweater over it – it's the only chair left, she'll have to sit there. Here's the candle – put it there too."

"Here she comes now. She's really slow – she's coming." The elephant was a large lump under the sweater.

Barbara soaked her biscotti in her coffee and took a bite. Then she swiped a piece of brownie from Gene's plate. He protested but was too involved with watching Grandma's slow progress to make a fuss. Grandma stopped in front of some fake Chinese pottery and then, catching a glimpse of the children watching her, she straightened up and moved on up the ramp.

"Grandma, Grandma, I got an elephant…" the noise was high. Barbara grabbed Amelia's hand and pinched it. Amelia shook her off but lowered her voice. "I got a little elephant to play with the pet rock, the book said it needed companions."

Barbara relaxed.

"And Barbara got an old book that has a lady with a tight skirt on the front and James said it was a good one, and the guys bought some old puzzles and a Rubber Cube…"

"Rubik's" said Gene.

And Grandma was at the top of the ramp and stopped, looking at the table of bouncing wiggling chattering people, all her people. It was Friday at last and the word was that the strike was over and she would have the weekend to do laundry and listen to the quiet. Perhaps she would tell Grandpoppa all about what happened, out loud, as if he sat across the table from her.

And she went to her chair and lifted Bab's sweater. And found the elephant. And the candle. And held it up with both hands. Barbara put the candle in the elephant's trunk. Then Esther smiled, a big loose smile that moved all the wrinkles around her mouth into laughter.

"It's beautiful," she said. "I'll eat in candlelight tonight."

THE VALKYRIES

1

It was mid-afternoon, a couple of hours before closing time, when Glenda stopped by Willie's table.

"Company?" she asked, plopping herself down next to Willie.

"Sure," said Willie. Willie and Glenda, manager of Monti's Café, were long-time buddies. Glenda shared Monti's gossip with Willie, and Willie shared stories, honed to a nicety, about their mutual acquaintances.

"You're hanging around late today," observed Glenda, whose day ran from 6 a.m. baking through 5 p.m. pot scrubbing.

"Yeah, Jake's playing golf and it's my day to cook." Willie's work day was shorter than Glenda's. "He always goes to the course early and if they play nine holes, that's two-plus hours, and then they go out for beer afterward. So lots of time on my hands. Guess I'll make a casserole or thaw some soup or something. Or maybe," Willi grinned at Glenda, "I'll take the left-over chili, half-price."

"Welcome to whatever's in the pot," said Glenda. "Should be plenty."

"You're not in the kitchen," Willie said. "Not closin' early?"

"Nah," said Glenda. "I had a late night last night, and the pantry is full. The girls can handle the rest of the day. I had to get off my feet."

"Late night?" asked Willie.

"Dancing!" said Glenda. "Man, if that guy had brains in his head as well as his feet, he'd be a keeper."

"Asking too much," said Willie. "Guys don't multitask. Sometimes they don't even task."

Bashing men in general was as easy as talking about the weather. Willie always made a couple of mental exceptions, but couldn't resist the snarky quip.

"You really should pick up some chili," said Glenda. "There's an endless pot, just for us non-cooks."

"Non-cooks! That's on my bucket list," said Willi. "I hate to cook – remember that the *I Hate to Cook Book* from the 60s?"

Glenda laughed. She knew that Willie had a perfectly nice husband who did a lot of cooking. He had a limited set of skills, though, so Willie brought him to Monti's when she couldn't stand another hot dog. He was a good tipper.

"So what about you – do you get tired of eating café food?" asked Willie.

"Not very often," said Glenda. "And when I do, somebody down in Montavilla will trade me a dinner. Or I scramble a couple of eggs and a chop. No one depends on me throwing together a dinner at 8 o'clock at night," Glenda added.

"Yeah, it was kind of a shock when Jake first moved in and we had to figure out who did what. I'm pretty casual," said Willie, gesturing toward her jeans and tatty sweatshirt, "and

Jake likes things just so. So first thing I had to do was persuade him that 'just so' meant 'just so I'm happy.' " She laughed. "It was my house, so I had that to bargain with. And he's a good egg. I hate to admit it, but I'm coming around to his notion of tidiness –I even carry my dishes to the sink when I'm through eating."

Glenda shook her head. "So you didn't have a live-in before Jake?"

"Oh I was married twice before and also had a long-time partner before Jake," said Willie, taking a swig of her mimosa, "So I'm used to dealing with men. By the time Jake came along, I decided I was tired of training men to my liking. So I told him it was my way or the highway. He just laughed and said he liked my big TV, so we're good."

Willie's speech was practiced, a bit sardonic.

"Two husbands," said Glenda, "I'd never have guessed."

"Three, actually," admitted Willie. "Jake and I are legal, although it may have been for taxes as much as love. Neither of us worry much what the neighbors think –" and then, another practiced line – "I'm not likely to get pregnant, so that takes care of that."

Glenda snorted. Willie was 75 years old.

"Well, I never got hitched even once," said Glenda, "although there were a couple of close calls. My live-ins got kicked out if they so much as asked me to turn on the tea kettle. My house, my rules."

Willie looked at Glenda. Glenda always seemed to have it together. She was flashy dresser with wonderful curves, probably in her mid-fifties. Her clothes fit her personality – solid and sparkling. She had good people working for her – Willie always figured that a good staff meant a good boss. Glenda's servers stayed around forever.

Willie said something to the effect that keeping the café happy was probably about as much as one human should have to do. Husbands were extras and took up a lot of space and effort.

"Yeah," said Glenda. "Even live-ins expand to fill the territory."

"So," Glenda continued, "Got any kids?"

Willie took another gulp of mimosa. "Yeah. Two. I don't see them very often."

"Oh, that's too bad. I mean," Glenda stopped, apologetically. "I didn't mean to pry. I guess it's too bad if it is too bad, if you know what I mean."

"Oh, it's OK," said Willie. "The oldest comes to Portland a couple of times a year." Her face opened up a bit. "She was here a few weeks ago. You might have seen her – she's, well, she's about your age or a little older, I think, dark hair, pretty eyes. A really nice person. She has a great job. I'm proud of her, we had a good visit."

"Oh I do remember the two of you together. You were both talking away like old buddies. I hadn't seen that side of you. Hm, I'm losing it. I usually can spot visiting relatives."

"Yeah, we were really close when she was little," said Willie. "My first husband, Toby, left when she was about three and her sister was under a year, so it felt like us against the world. Although Elizabeth, when she was here, reminded me of all the relatives who showed up when the cupboard was bare. They brought candy for the kids. My favorite brother, workin' as a logger in the Coast Range – those were the days of the big logging boom – Johnny, bless him, put aside some of his paycheck every week and stuck it under our door. So we didn't starve or freeze.

"We had some good times, even though I couldn't stretch the weekly paycheck much past five days. I worked at the five-and-dime and then waitressed a little on the side and got to take home left-overs" – Willie smiled at Glenda – "the kids liked that. We had pennies for the gum machine and there was a nice little park in town -- we lived down the valley, in Roseburg -- with swings and sliding boards and a zoo of sorts that was free. We managed, maybe better without Tiresome Toby."

Glenda laughed. "Tiresome Toby"– what was his problem?"

"Well, to be fair, he was mostly just young, 17 when we got married. So was I but kids will grow you up pretty quick. He came home one day, all worn out from work, and the kids jumped all over him, "Daddy Daddy Daddy.' He put them down on the couch, went to the bedroom, packed a duffle bag and told me – I was making grilled cheese for supper – that he was leaving. And he did.

"I didn't mind him going – he didn't contribute much to the cookie jar, what with gas and ammunition and the amount he ate – but it was hard on the girls, especially on Elizabeth. Ashley was too little to understand, but Elizabeth thought it was her fault. I had to figure out ways to make her understand it was his bad boss and the broken-down car that he wanted to get away from. I even lied and told the two of them that someday he'd come back. But he never has."

Willie looked down at her glass. The gumball machine and biggest sliding board had almost persuaded Elizabeth that it was OK and that she hadn't chased her daddy away. Or at least that's what Elizabeth had told her when she visited.

"Well, Elizabeth looked really happy when she was gabbing away with you," said Glenda, squirming a little. Willie figured Glenda didn't want to know too much bad stuff about her customers' lives – too much bad stuff floating around. Probably had some bad times herself.

Glenda asked, "How did you get to Portland – did the girls go to school here?"

"Well, that's another story. Here, let me get you another mimosa. I'll have another too – that was my first and I'm on foot."

Bridget Clare was at the counter and took the two mimosa orders. Willie liked her. She was big across the shoulders, soft spoken, close friends with Glenda. They had worked together at Monti's for years.

"Here you go, Willie. And hey, keep Glenda talking – she needs a little time off from scrubbing pots and bossing us around." Bridget Clare smiled to let Willie know she wasn't dissing her boss.

Willie carried the mimosas back to the table slowly. She had grown up with "we don't talk about it" folks and thought it was best to let sleeping dragons lie, but Glenda's interest in her was making her forget her caution. She really didn't want to talk about the years of the kids growing up. Portland was easier.

"Portland was a big city after Roseburg," she said. "I got to dance like a fool when I came to the city."

"Dancing!" said Glenda. "I love to dance. Portland's great for those weekend swing gigs -- you can even find good, old-fashioned cheek-to-cheek stuff."

"Jake and I used to dance a lot," said Willie. "In fact, the first time we saw each other was at a dance club down in the city – Lola's."

"Oh I love Lola's – and the McMenamins is right there too." Glenda perked up at the thought. "Did you ever go to the great tango place – what's it called -- Berretin?"

"Well, Llewelyn and I took some tango lessons, but it wasn't Jake's thing. He liked line dancing and Salsa, though." Willie smiled. "I was with Llewelyn when I first met Jake. I thought he – Jake, I mean -- was a nice nerd and I didn't see him again for, um, close to five years."

Bridget Clare came up to Glenda to ask a question about closing out the cookie counter. Glenda glanced at her, smiled, and said that she and Willie were talking about men and dancing.

"Tell her about your frying pan," said Bridget Clare. She turned to Willie. "I love that story – Glenda tells it well. It isn't exactly about dancing, although I guess," Bridget Clare looked thoughtful, "you might include it in a general notion of how the tango works domestically."

Glenda laughed, a sound that came from deep inside her and then turned into a giggle. "Oh baby," she said to Bridget Clare, "that's a good one. The tango at home, with a frying pan – position the hands for the grip, get your feet in an open stance for balance, and concentrate on the shoulder swing."

Willie smiled, enjoying the two women's joking, even as she didn't understand. "The frying pan move? That's a new one to me," she said.

Bridget Clare tapped Glenda on the shoulder and said, "tell her." And went back to the kitchen.

"Well," said Glenda, turning to Willie, "Well, the story is about one of my live-ins. This was, oh probably 20 years ago – I was a mere child of 30 and this handsome guy came on to me and we hooked up. Turned out he was an abuser and hard to get rid of. I mean, after a few months he was choosing clothes for me – granny clothes that I would never wear – and not letting me go out with my girlfriends on Friday nights. Well, that lasted for a little while and then one night he took a swing at me – after we'd been drinking, of course – and I remembered what me dear ol' Ma said to Daddy – this is a family legend.

"Early in my parents' marriage, Mom said, when she and Dad were still sorting things out – that is, by arguing and fighting through their differences -- Mom thought Dad was getting too, um, physical. She said she picked up a frying pan from the stove – she'd been cooking when the yelling began. She held it up, just for a minute, and then sat it down on the hot burner where the oil started to smoke.

"Then she said very slowly – and when Dad told the story, he made her sound like one of those deadly goddesses – she said, slowly: 'You have to sleep sometime.'

"Daddy always told that story on himself. After that, he said, he could end their arguments by saying, 'Can I go sleep now?' and that always made her laugh."

Willie snorted. "Did your live-in stick around and sleep?" she asked. She had never imagined Glenda, so competent and handsome, having a bad lover.

"Nope, he was gone the next morning. And I think he had a bad night, too," said Glenda.

"Wish I had known that trick," said Willie.

"Ah, you had one of those – legal? I hope not," said Glenda.

"It's harder to get rid of them when it's legal. And they always like your salary, even if they don't like your attitude."

Willie gulped a little. "Yeah," she said, "You got it there. Dick was one of the worst SOBs I ever ran into. He was handsome and a good talker and I thought the girls could use a daddy. So I got hitched to his broken down wagon. With him, it was always a load of manure."

Willie used the "manure wagon" to describe her life with the Dickhead. It generally stopped the conversation, which is what she intended.

There are some things people just don't talk about.

Except Glenda was 20 years younger, so she didn't know she should change the subject.

"So that was #2, after what's his face, young Tiresome, disappeared?" Glenda asked.

The mimosa was having its way with Willie.

"Ah yeah, Dick and I got married. He was a logger, gone a good part of the year, so I was slow to figure out how bad he was. By the time he started to smack me around, we had a little house and the kids were doing well in school and liked having nice clothes. And the people there in Roseburg, they were a good lot, considering. The preacher sometimes came to check on us – he called it a pastoral visit – and he'd leave money behind the coffee pot. We didn't talk about Dick, but he saw my bruises. His wife would take the girls home with her on weekends.

"Anyway, Dick started drinking on the job, which is a big no-no – logging is dangerous even when you're sober – but it was more than just the beer and whiskey with him, he got sorta nuts. I was frantic, what with work and the kids and all. Luckily, by the time he went completely off his head, Elizabeth was working at the Coast. And," Willie looked down at her almost empty glass, "Ashley had left home – she went off to LA in tenth grade and stayed with a cousin of mine. During the worst times the neighbors would warn me at work that Dick was home. I'd stay with my sister or brother, until one day he got out his gun and started shooting dogs and howling – well, it took a couple of times – and they arrested him and decided he was off his rocker. Long story short – he got put in the State Hospital up in Salem, the insane asylum." Willie looked away. "Ashley didn't want to have anything to do with me or Oregon but she kept in touch with Elizabeth. She, Ashley, was safe in LA."

"I'll never forget." Willie took a big gulp of her mimosa and looked back at Glenda. "I was running the cash register when the manager came out and said he'd got a phone call from the hospital, telling him to tell me that Dick was dead. I was just stopped. I couldn't close the register drawer. I was a stone. Apparently, I made a weird noise, and the other girls came over and took over the register and somebody took me to the storage room and brought me water – they thought I was, like, bowled over by grief. I laughed crazy-like and then couldn't stop bawling, and they gave me Kleenex and sent me home for the day.

"The truth is, after the first shock, I was floating, like. I was light, outside myself, like someone pulled a Doug fir off my back. And worse, later that night, I got to be glad he was dead. You never should be glad about anybody's dying -- but I was. That's really sinful, to be happy someone is dead like I was.

"I went to Dick's getting buried – they put him in one of those graves for people who can't afford a regular cemetery – but neither of the girls showed up for the 'services.' I got a lot of shit over that – 'their daddy is their blood' and all that – but of course, he wasn't. I never told anybody how glad I was. 'You have to sleep sometime,' " she repeated. "I should have known about that."

The two women drank off the last of their mimosas, Glenda said she had to get back to work, and Willie wandered back toward home. She sat down on a bench at Berrydale Park, and wondered why she had told Glenda about Dick. No one except Jake knew about that marriage – and no one, until Glenda, had asked. It felt good that she got to tell someone how that life was long gone.

Of course, Glenda would probably forget all about Willie's story. Willie was just another old lady with a history of mistakes. She got up from the park bench, picked a couple of dandelions, and went home to make Jake some grilled cheese.

2

The next time Willie showed up at Monti's, the place was packed. Alyssa, The Rev's wife, was sitting by herself at a table for two. The Rev was at a table in a far corner listening to a bedraggled-looking woman. Alyssa invited Willie to take the chair across from her.

"Hey old lady, how's it going?" Alyssa always greeted Willie as "old lady." It made Willie laugh. Alyssa older than Willie. She had a smudge of blue paint beside her nose.

"Doin' good," said Willie. "How's the painting going? You must be working on skies." Reaching up to her face, Willie tapped her finger on her cheek.

Alyssa reached up and rubbed her face. "Did I get some paint on me?" she asked. "Oh mercy, I need Jimmy. He tells me when I'm mucky." Jimmy was The Rev, a pastor at a little church down the street. He used Monti's for pastoral outreach. Alyssa was strictly forbidden to say as much as a hello when The Rev was officially counseling.

"It's nothing," said Willie. "Here, let me wipe it off." Willie reached up with a napkin and gingerly wiped at the smudge. It lightened a bit, and Alyssa smiled and said thanks.

"So," said Alyssa, "What's up on your side of town?"

"Not a whole lot," said Willie. "Jake's sleeping through golf on the TV. I snuck out. Since it's his turn to cook, I'm off the hook."

Alyssa laughed. "Glenda sneaked out of Monti's the other day – it was noon and she was dressed to the nines," she said. "Probably going dancing."

"She's probably working on a competition. I hear she's really good," said Willie.

"Do you and Jake dance?" asked Alyssa.

Dancing seemed to be a hot topic at Monti's these days.

"Not anymore," said Willie. "We used to but he has an ear problem that makes him dizzy. When he couldn't take me out to tango any more, he tried to teach me to golf. We gave that up fast. I could throw those darn little balls through a basketball hoop, but I never got the hang of hitting them with a club. So now we mostly weed and sleep together."

Alyssa laughed. "I never could get Jimmy to dance except in the line of duty. I told him it was his duty toward me, but his dancing was so wretched it wasn't worth it. So there's this old gent at church who likes to dance, and he and his wife and Jimmy and I meet up once in a while so I can get the kinks out."

"What kind of dancing?" asked Willie.

"Oh I love the salsa and the tango. Jimmy is only good for the two-step but the old church guy really does a pretty tango. He can't go on for long, but when he goes, it's awesome."

"I always loved the tango," said Willie. "I wasn't very good, but Llewelyn – he came before Jake – was a whiz. I could even feel that sense of 'cosmic necessity' – that's what he called it – when I got some of the moves just right. Pretty awesome."

"So who's Llewelyn? Sounds like your kind of guy," Alyssa said.

"Weelll," said Willie, drawing out her words. Llewelyn was her secret power, the man who insisted she was a Willie, not a Wilma, and stood by her at the courthouse when she got her name changed. Llewelyn taught her, Willie, that she was an alright human being.

"Well, yeah, he was my special guy," said Willie. "I met him after my second husband died, down in Roseburg. Llewelyn had a job with the state board of education – the southern Willamette Valley was his territory – and when he was in town, he ate at the restaurant where I worked.

"That food joint was a pretty rough place, especially when the loggers were off work – I could usually handle them, but sometimes things got out of hand. One night – I was in my forties at the time and not what you'd call hot – this one guy, whenever I got near him, kept sliding his hand up my skirt. I was cool until he got too close to the target, if you know what I mean."

Willie looked at Alyssa and grinned. "I jumped away from him and 'accidentally' poured the coffee I was carrying into his lap. The fellow screamed, the dining room went dead silent, and then he called me the, the C word." Willie rolled her eyes."

"He stumbled out of his chair – he was pretty drunk – to come after me. I reached over to another table and grabbed a water pitcher, ready to sling it at him, and then suddenly -- there was Llewelyn. Llewelyn –" Willie lingered on the name, "Llewelyn had been sitting at the next table over and by the time the guy was on his feet, Llewelyn was standing between us, staring at him. The other guys at the table started laughing 'cause the creep looked like he peed his pants, and Llewelyn didn't say anything, he just stood there until the drunk slid back down into his chair and the place got noisy again and the creep's friends started razzing him. Then my boss came out and everyone settled down and she took over the table. I went back into the kitchen and the girls and I did some of our own swearing."

"When we closed up, Llewelyn was waiting at the restaurant door. He even took off his hat to me – as if I didn't smell of dead grease and onions – and said he was going my way and would I like company? I was happy for the company – it was a dark night. We'd had friendly exchanges before, and he'd lent me a book about a famous basketball player, but until that night I figured he was just another lonely traveler.

"So that was the beginning. Turned out he was a bachelor, tall, good-lookin' and soft of voice. Everyone knew him and liked him.

"Oh ho," said Alyssa. "Your restaurant sounds like Mel's, in that movie, what was it? '*Alice Doesn't Live Here Anymore?*' Where the hard-bitten waitress is asked where the F is the cook and she says…"

"He went out back …" chimed in Willie.

"To take a shit," said Alyssa.

"And the hogs et' him." Willie finished it off.

Then she added – "But they didn't use the F word in movies back then."

The two women laughed loud enough that The Rev raised his head to them and smiled, just a little. "Jimmy and I love that movie – we even bought the DVD when it came out."

"Oh yeah," said Willie, "Llewelyn and I saw it three times in a row. Roseburg was a Clint Eastwood town, so it took a while for Alice to get there, but the first time we saw it, we had to go back. And again! Cemented our relationship real good."

"Anyway, the rest of the story, Llewelyn got transferred to Portland and asked if I wanted to join him here and I did. He loved Portland, knew all the funny little cafes and parks and dance places. We had a wonderful 20 years or so. Then he up and died on me."

Alyssa put her hand on Willie's. "That's – I'm so sorry. He sounds like a gem." Alyssa looked at the back corner, where The Rev still sat. "My Jimmy is my gem – I've been really lucky. We found each other when I was thirty, and we are still getting along pretty good." Alyssa smiled through her sympathy.

Willie smiled back. The Rev was a good man and lucky to have Alyssa, just as she was lucky to have him.

"It was Llewellyn's heart," Willie said. "We had 20 years of good times, and then he was gone. He left me the house he had bought, and I got part of his pension, but I fell apart for a while. A couple of years."

"And then I had a kitchen fire – wiring was old -- and this guy came to rewire, and before I knew it he had cleaned up the kitchen, was mowing the lawn, and bringing me sandwiches. I started to crawl out of the hole that Llewelyn's death put me in, and, of course, the handyman was Jake, who, in his own steady way, talked me into going back out into the world. We danced some and he started to stay over, and then he moved in. We got married a few years back 'cause it made taxes easier. And here we are."

Alyssa sat quiet for a minute.

"The universe comes through sometimes," she said quietly. "And hey, here comes Jimmy," Alyssa's voice brightened. "you have to tell him about the salsa and how much easier it is than the tango. I'm still trying to get his feet untangled."

And so the conversation went back to safe ground.

On her way home, Willie thought, not for the first time, about how Monti's was a – what did they call it now? – a safe space. Elizabeth, she thought, would be proud of her, talking about bad times and putting them safely into stories.

3

A few days later, Willie and Alyssa met at Berrydale Park. Willie was on her way to Monti's and Alyssa was walking off the excitement of having finished a life-sized portrait of Jimmy. Alyssa had on paint-covered blue jeans and an old flannel shirt. Her fingernails showed purple in the cuticles. She looked tired but happy.

The two women decided to meander to Monti's and celebrate the finished painting.

"Jimmy," Alyssa declared, "is home reading about the Big Bang which he says didn't happen."

"Well, I could tell him of several small bangs, if he needed them," said Willie, snorting.

At Monti's, they found themselves a table in the nearly deserted dining room. They waved at the two women doing dishes behind the counter. Willie went to order chips and salsa and a couple of mimosas. The young woman, Kim, at the counter suggested brownies to go with the mimosas. She and Willie joked about calorie counts and excess sugar.

"Can't do champagne *and* chocolate," said Willie. "So champagne comes first."

Kim laughed and pulled the change from the cash register.

Behind Willie, a big man with an oversized gut pushed through the Monti doors. He was dressed in jeans and a T-shirt. Willie caught a whiff of stale beer. She glanced back at him as he came up behind her and then turned to take the bills from Kim. The young woman, clutching the bills, held them in midair and stepped backwards. Willie felt a shove and stumbled a bit to the right. She grabbed the pastry display cabinet and turned toward the man standing where she had been a minute ago. He had his hands flat on the counter, glaring at Kim.

"Bitch," he yelled. "Where are the keys? And my dinner. I told you I was going to go in early today."

The bills in Kim's hand shook. Her voice trembled. "The keys are on the stand by the door. I left them there for you. I didn't have time, I was late. You can eat here – I'll fix something for you."

"No! I don't like the goddamn food in this joint," he said. "And if you got out of bed sooner, I'd be eating right now."

He leaned over the counter, his hands, crusted with dirt, angled toward her. Kim backed up against the sink. A staff member looked around the corner from the kitchen and ducked out of sight.

Willie was rigid. The beer smell was strong. She glanced at the counter beside her and noted a half-full water pitcher. She moved her right hand toward it.

Alyssa came from the dining room. Willie saw her out of the corner of her eye. "Call the cops," Willie said.

Then she turned toward the guy, facing him squarely, and used her shoulders to get a good hold on the heavy, ice-filled pitcher.

"You! What do you think you are doing? Get out!" Willie's voice surprised her. She lifted the pitcher, fixing it so she could swing it at him, using her full body weight.

The man turned toward her. Behind him Bridget Clare came through the kitchen door. "They're coming – called 911" she yelled.

"Out!" Willie pointed at the door. "Do you hear me? If you wanta eat, catch a muskrat in the swamp you came out of."

The man stared at Willie. His face turned red and he glared back at Kim. Another server from the kitchen had come in and stood behind her. Bridget Clare moved to one side of the man, where he could see the cast iron frying pan she held in both hands. Another server came up behind her. From the dining room a woman appeared, phone raised, taking a video. Outside a siren wailed.

The big guy looked all around, then took a step forward. Willie decided to pitch the ice water and then hit him with the heavy pitcher. Bridget Clare would back her up.

"Bitches!" he yelled, looking first at Willie and then at Bridget Clare. He glared at Kim behind the counter but turned to the door. He caught his toe on the threshold and stumbled. Bridget Clare followed, just behind.

"Don't let the door hit you in the ass," she yelled.

He regained his balance, staggered, half-running to an old pick-up truck slewed sideways in the street. He turned and yelled toward the café: "Cunts!" Then he roared off.

The women looked at one another.

"Bridget Clare! Would you really have hit him?" Willie asked.

Bridget Clare shook her head. "I don't know," she said, "but yeah, maybe I would have. Willie, you sounded like my Mom – just like my Mom."

Bridget Clare put the frying pan down and went to the young woman behind the cash register. She took the money from Kim's hand and passed it to Willie. The women behind the counter surrounded Kim and started talking. "Man, he was some shit," one of them said.

"Yeah," said another. "Did you see how fast he took off. He must be in a lot of trouble. I saw the cops go after him." She put her arm around Kim and the two of them went into the kitchen. The other server nodded at Willie, giving her a thumbs up and returned to making the mimosas.

Alyssa stood a little ways away. "That was awesome," she said. "Willie, you old dear, that was awesome."

Willie gulped. "That was downright scary," she said.

"That too," said Alyssa.

"Will she be alright?" asked Willie, gesturing toward the kitchen where she could hear murmurs from the staff.

"They'll take care of her," said Alyssa. "I'll give Glenda a call. She knows the right people. They won't let her go home."

"That guy will think first before he takes on little old ladies who know a thing or two," she said. "He ran faster than a rat trying to escape his fleas."

Willie shook her head and laughed out loud. And the two women took their mimosas back to their table.

WEDNESDAYS AT MONTI'S

I

That Wednesday, Willie sat by herself in a mostly empty Monti's Café. Aylssa was attending an Iowa conference of Small Christian Communities with Helen, the church lady. Alyssa had taken over her husband's preaching position when his heart acted up. Magdalena, who gave up her floating silks for camping gear, was with Ralph, glacier-gazing in Canada. The Rev was home, presumably studying up on new galaxies. And the two sisters who shepherded their mom weren't around much anymore. The last time Willie had seen them, in July, Mama argued she needed her two coats and three sweaters.

So, a quiet afternoon at the café. Only V, an older woman, sat next to the window, across the aisle from Willie. V was alone.

Ordinarily V would have been with a man, also in his 80s, clearly a longtime friend or husband. The pair were always absorbed in each other's conversations. V, a loud talker, was oblivious to other café goers. Her guy was quieter and noticed more of his surrounds. Sometimes he smiled at Willie.

V's guy always brought her her coffee, took it back for more cream, ordered mimosas and carried them to her, and then fetched the fork she forgot. He waited on her, and V seemed to take him for granted.

But V also responded to him. When he read aloud from his phone, V would frown or laugh raucously. She would joke with him or even, so it appeared to Willie, correct him, always checking to make sure he was OK with her bumptious opinions.

But now, V had begun to show up by herself. She would sit, stiff and silent in her chair, checking her phone and nursing a warm, flat mimosa.

On this particular afternoon, V sat in her usual place, silent and self-absorbed. At one point, she reached for her phone and caught her mimosa glass with the back of her hand. It sprayed across the aisle onto Willie's table, splashing Willie's jeans. The glass broke into tiny pieces. Monti's staff came running with brooms and mops. Willie grabbed a bunch of napkins and cleaned herself up. Then she got clean napkins for V who sat, as if frozen, in her chair.

"I'm sorry," V said, looking at the bunch of napkins that Willie was handing her but not taking them. "Thank you."

V's voice felt strange to her. She felt outside the scene, observing it. Was she at fault? What had struck her glass? Should she be doing something? A new mimosa appeared in front of her. A figure across the table shoved napkins at the remaining mimosa drops.

"Whew! What a mess.," said Willie. "All that sugar." V saw Willie looking at her. V still couldn't understand what was going on.

"Here – have another mimosa," said Willie. "You look like you could use it."

"Thank you," replied V, again. "You, you shouldn't have.... I..." V couldn't think what she should have done.

Willie smiled and said, "No problem. You look like you needed a drink."

"I guess I do," said V. "Here, let me get this." V sat motionless, her hands still in her lap, not reaching for her purse.

"Nah, what's a mimosa or two among fellow travelers," said Willie, looking at the fixed figure across the table. "Where's your guy these days, anyway?" Willie was wiping off V's phone as she asked.

V looked at her. "My guy?" she said.

"The gentleman you usually come in with – you haven't broken up, have you?" Willie tightened her lips and frowned.

"He's at home." V said. Then she said, louder: "In bed. My daughter's sitting with him."

"Not feeling well?" asked Willie?

"As well as can be expected," said V, "on chemo."

Willie grimaced. She recognized V's inability to react. "I'm sorry. I'm really sorry. I had noticed that you were coming in by yourself, but I had no idea…."

"That's OK." V replied slowly. "Caddie – our daughter – is with him. She comes on Wednesdays and makes me get out of the house." V continued, "I tried walking until Caddie let me come home, but my knees can't handle more than a couple blocks.

"He's doing OK, you know," aid V, turning her face toward the window. "As well as can be expected."

Willie shook her head. "That's not good," she said.

"No." V turned back to Willie "Not good, actually. But it's all I have to report." V shrugged and put her hands back in her lap.

Willie opened her book, which she had grabbed out of the way of the flying mimosa, and said, "Do you know anything about lace-making?"

"Lace-making?" asked V, trying to pay attention.

"Yeah, I saw this book – it's from the 1800s, I mean, on lace-making in Ceylon. You know, eastern Asia. Where the Brits went when they were still great."

V frowned. "Lace-making in Ceylon," she said.

"Yeah – here, listen, 'Chapter 1: Concerning the History of Lace-making in the World; Chapter 2: Providing a History of Lace-making in Ceylon; Chapter 3: Wherein the Most Important Lace-makers in Ceylon are discovered and interrogated; Chapter 4: Regarding The Oceanic Commerce Bringing Ceylonese Lace to the British Isles; Chapter 5: the Improvement of Ceylonese Laces through British and Continental Lace-making Techniques.'

"I mean, you don't have to read the book to know everything about Ceylon lace-making you'll ever want to know." Willie closed the book. "I'm Willie, by the way."

V smiled suddenly and shook her head. "And I'm V. But those are weird chapter heads –I mean, they're like 'Chapter 1 Wherein Doris Eats her Oats.'" V sat up a bit straighter and looked directly at Willie.

Willie covered her mouth with her hand: "John Lennon!" Willie stared at V. But it's, it's 'Where Doris *Gets* her Oats.'"

"Oh right. Yeah, 'gets'," said V. "But it was McCartney, not Lennon who wrote it." V looked closer at Willie. "How'd you know about that?"

'Oh I don't know," said Willie. "I was a Beatles fan – am a Beatles fan. It's on *Let It Be*, right? And it's "gets her oats" because it's about sex – you know, the female sowing her wild oats and such-like. It's Lennon who sings it, I think, but McCartney who wrote it. Or maybe the other way around. And they were about to break up."

V knew that Willie was talking about the Beatles, not Doris and her man.

"Oh my." V gave a great sigh. "It's been years: 'On our way home. On our way home.'"

And just like that, the two old women found subjects to carry on about. V told Willie about Moll Flanders, the heroine of an old novel with click-bait subheads. She quoted from memory:

"*The Fortunes and Misfortunes of the Famous Moll Flanders Who was born in Newgate, and during a life of continu'd Variety for Threescore Years, besides her Childhood, was Twelve Years a Whore, five times a Wife (whereof once to her brother) Twelve Years a Thief, Eight Years a Transported Felon in Virginia, at last grew Rich, liv'd Honest and died a Penitent – Written from her own Memorandums.*

"Newgate was the jail – in those days, they laid it all out," said V. "Didn't worry about spoilers." V laughed out loud.

"How the hell did you recite that?" Willie asked. "It's not exactly the King's English."

"First time I read it, in college," V said, "I thought it was hilarious. I was 21 and eager to know how to live -- and here was the blueprint. That was over 60 years ago – but I haven't been in jail yet."

V couldn't have dredged up that quote if she had been asked to, but with the help of mimosas and Willie's funny eager face, it came back to her.

Willie then recited to V the sports events that her guy, Jake, could watch in a single day – pre-season basketball, football training camp, baseball game, golf, and in a pinch, cricket. "And then he can recite to me not just the scores but the highlights of each of the events, with side snarks about the commentators."

"At least," said Willie, "Old Moll died at the end. ESPN goes on forever." And the two women grinned at each other.

II

The next Wednesday Willie saw V, still alone, going into Monti's; she grabbed V before V could put in her order. "Come on. We're going for a walk."

V looked at Willie, as if slowly recalling who she was.

Willie insisted, "We'll come back here afterward. You need to get out."

V stood still and shook her head a little. "I can't walk much. Arthritis. Besides, he had a bad night. I need my coffee."

"OK, we'll get it." Willie turned to the cashier and ordered two French roasts, to go. The coffee was handed over, and Willie ushered the objecting V out the door.

"I don't want to do this, you know," said V.

"I know. But you need to get out. Didn't your daughter tell

you? And it's August and the sun is shining and it's not too hot. You can cuss at me while we walk. It will do you good." Willie took V's arm, gently moving her down the sidewalk.

The two women walked slowly through the neighborhood south of Monti's. It was an old suburb of small houses with lawns bordered in juniper and rhododendron. It was a post-W.W.II development, cheap-built for newly-wed GIs. It had grown into its eccentricities over the following 70 years and now had a slip-shod charm. Willie loved the way the houses differed, having bumped out rooms, bay windows, added chimneys.

V was indifferent. Her knees hurt and Willie walked too fast. Willie slowed her own footsteps to match V's.

"There's a big yellow cat called Fluffy that usually lies under that bush," said Willie. "She'll flick her ears at us if we speak.

"And a couple of kids live next door. They have a trampoline and like to show off. I call them 5, 6, and 7, even though they are 10, 11, and 12 now. They challenge me to a jumping contest. Not around today – probably at the kite-making camp at the park."

"Can we go back now?" said V.

"Nope, not much further. We have to turn onto Market and then go up 85th a bit. Just two more blocks," said Willie.

V didn't respond but she found herself looking around. Being a caregiver had blinded her to everything but keeping the house together and Conrad clean and fed. V had a long-standing loyalty to the neighborhoods near Monti's, cut into pieces by a federal interstate and a busy state highway. The old suburb may have seen better times – but maybe -- maybe these were its best times. It was full of life, perked up by the crazed diversity of houses, honed with decades of changing lives. V, in spite of herself, made note of doors in shades of red – tomato, fire engine, magenta? Cinnabar, vermillion? She always loved a red door.

V remembered her knees. "How much further," she asked.

Willie gestured: "Almost there."

"Where are we going, anyway?" said V.

V's irritation pleased Willie. It was a sign she was paying attention. "To the Twin Pines Country Club," said Willie.

"There's no country club around here." V said.

"That's what they call it – the Twin Pines Country Club," said Willie. "You know, 'Keep Portland weird.' "

"You mean, it's a real place?" V asked.

"Yup. Right here in this low-class neighborhood," said Willie.

"You mean working class – low income, right?" V responded. Her progressive politics and aching knees made her sound snarky.

And then Willie opened up both arms, presenting V with her gift.

They were facing a small, one story house on a large lot. The front, longer side of the house had two-100 foot Douglas fir trees, one at each end of a carved up, weed-and path strewn lawn. The yard plants were all dun-colored stalks, bowed by age and heavy with seeds. Snaking through the grasses were paths of green, outdoor carpet, laid flat and lined with bright red bricks.

"A maze!" said V.

"Nope." Willie beamed. "It's a golf course. Look at the hole in the Easter Island thingie!" She pointed to one end of the intertwined paths. Sure enough, a concrete copy of an Eastern Island head had an oval opening through its center bottom.

"Oh – oh. A miniature golf course. Miniature golf. Of course. Some old guy's thumbing his nose at the country club set. The Twin Pines, the Country Club. How funny!" V said.

"Oh no, not at all," said Willie. "Jake and I come here a lot. The couple who did this are about 30 years old, hiking-and-camping types. The kids, probably first and second graders, have a lemonade stand. And someone stole some of the statues, so the neighbors donated extra heavy ones like those two gold-painted lions. They weigh about 500 pounds each."

V shook her head. "The kids? – do children live here?"

"It's a family – look at the statues of the kissing Dutch children – aren't they cute? And the windmill, of course. They have a phone app for an online score card. And you can get clubs and balls from the box by texting for the key combination. It's a hoot!"

Two young girls appeared at the edge of the beige house. Willie waved to them. One of the kids was dressed mostly in a cape of a super hero. The other stood smiling in a puffy tutu. They waved and then disappeared into the house. When they reappeared, the older one was carrying a pitcher of murky yellowish liquid and the younger balancing paper cups.

"Would you like some lemonade?" The young one spoke in a high-pitched, rehearsed voice. "We give the proceeds to the park fund. You may have it for free if you can't pay. But we urge you to be generous. It's only $1 a glass. Or" she added, "you can bring your money back later. We can't take credit cards – Mom said no way."

And then she added, "We really really like the park and we might be able to get some new slides or somethin' if we make enough money. It's kind of beat-up, and the swings don't have seats but new stuff would make it more fun."

Willie said "Sure." And bought two glasses, adding a $5 tip to a jar.

V sat down on one of the big boulders that formed a wall around the yard. The lemonade was sweet, cold, and wet. The children were charming. And Willie chatted as the older girl got a putter out of the box. Willie swung it with practiced moves, knocking a ball between the two lions. V watched, silent.

She could recount this scene to Conrad. He would love to hear how the paths meandered, how the windmill bounced the balls back at the players, and the way everyone had access. V imagined a parent, peering through a window, keeping an eye on the strangers.

"Can't take the time to play a real game now." Willie handed the club back to the younger one. "Gotta get this old lady back to Monti's for more coffee."

"Monti's has good cookies," said the smaller child, gesturing at V. "The old lady has wonderful hair. It would make good fairy hair." The little girl smiled at V, who found herself smiling back. And with Willie's help, V rose from the rock, and the two of them turned, and went back up the street to the cafe.

III

And so, a routine was established. The women called it their "Old Lady Adventures" and made it a regular thing.

They went first to the Puppet Museum (V's suggestion) and then to a trendy boutique full of skeletons, mounted deer heads, and boxes of rocks (Willie's choice). They wandered around Movie Madness's Museum and Willie drove them to the Reed College Canyon, where they talked to the ducks. They checked out the rhododendron gardens, which had flowers in August as well as May. They visited a warehouse called "My Memories" which had, among a mountain of other things, a wall of old radios and political campaign buttons. Willie said that the warehouse felt exactly like her memories -- no themes, no meanings, just stuff and more stuff. V said that it was much like Willie's conversations. Then she felt guilty about being snarky. Willie laughed.

Then a gentle game of one-ups-man-ship began. V suggested Mary's Club, a tacky, sorta-feminist, strip club downtown, but Willie said no, not unless they went to the Bikini Baristas out on Division. They agreed that both places might be a bit too much. "I mean, what would we do when we got propositioned?" asked Willie.

One day V talked Willie into going to the Zymoglyphic Museum. "No more pretty flowers," she said. "Let's do something serious."

"The what museum?" asked Willie. "I thought we decided museums were too much." V had said she couldn't bear the "I don't know anything about art but I know what I like" school of museum-tourists.

"The Zymoglyphic Museum." V smiled a little. "First, it's in a garage – a big garage, so there's that. And second, it's not like art as you would think of it. And third, the guy who runs it made up the word 'zymoglyphic' so we don't have to be serious."

"Well," said Willie. "Well…." Then she shrugged. "OK. It's your choice. 'Garage' sounds like home. And making up words is something you would do and since I can stand you, I guess I can stand the zymo-whatever. You buy the mimosas when we get back."

Willie had V spell out the name of the museum, putting it on her phone. Later, Willie found a definition on Google:

"zy'-mo-glyph'-ic. 1. Of, or pertaining to, images of fermentation, specifically the solid residue of creative fermentation on natural objects. 2. The collection and arrangement of objects, primarily either natural or weathered by natural forces, for poetic effect."

Except for "poetic effect," Willie thought, the definition of the stuff at the museum could apply to the contents of her garage. Jake collected a lot of stuff, some of it oldish, rusty and splintered, like the walking stick branches he liked to pick up. Willie liked shiny rocks so they lined the garage walls. Her craft projects, crooked cups and dangly wire things, also decorated the space. Perhaps she and Jake could learn something about their Zymo potential. Willie decided it would be educational.

The two women met at Monti's and drove to a nearby neighborhood. The houses were large and multi-storied, set into the side of the hill leading to Mount Tabor Park.

Willie was enthralled with the architecture. She bounced a little as she walked, exclaiming over a carved gate and a wraparound porch with a view of Mt. Hood. "Jake and I always wanted to live up here," she said, "but we couldn't afford a dog house. These houses sure are nifty."

"Too much cleaning and too many stairs," said V. A couple of finches were shaking water off their wings beside a fountain.

"There it is!" said Willie.

They stood in front of a tall, many-windowed house with a garage under its three stories. A hand-printed sign announced "Zymoglyphic Museum." A narrow door opened to the sidewalk.

Willie hesitated. V limped ahead of her.

"Welcome," said a deep male voice from within.

Shaking off the sunshine, the two women stopped just inside the door. The air had a tang of rust and mold and dust.

Willie was bewildered by the dimness, stunned by heaps of unfathomable objects. Shelves, bookcases, and glassed-in aquariums were stuffed with unnameable things. A wide wooden desk, covered with papers, sat in the center of the confused materials. At the desk sat an older man. He was ordinary looking, graying hair, alert eyes, indifferent to the two elderly women in front of him. "Welcome," he said again, not looking up.

V smiled at him. He looked more closely at her. Willie, standing beside her, was not sure of what she was seeing and not happy with what she could identify.

The garage had 40 watt bulbs lighting walls crowded with humanoid figures and moss and skeletons of small beasts. Along the wall across from the desk were stacks of books and pamphlets in wire holders, interspersed with musty looking drapes of rusted wire and faded black backdrops.

"A phantasmagorum," announced V.

"Whatever…." Willie whispered.

"The exhibit hall is up the stairs, ladies. Please hold the railings as you advance. And watch your step – the stairs were handmade and are not always even."

"No admission price?" Willie moved reluctantly into the dim space. She felt she was disappearing, being enveloped in dust and cobwebs and becoming part of strange floating drapes, drooping from the ceiling. Everywhere she looked, the space was overfull of oozing figures, mucky and ugly.

Like Hades, Willie thought. Hell is blaring light. Hades is swamp, smothering slime.

"Not my style," announced V, standing just behind Willie. She sounded cheerful. "But this certainly echoes my nightmares." V's voice was loud and mocking. Willie didn't respond.

"The museum is arranged by themes," said the man behind the desk. "That may help you navigate it. Or not, as you wish. The themes are announced on the walls above the art. And you can find a definition of zymoglyphic on the walls as well."

He went back to his book. He had an old lamp, green with a goose neck. It barely illuminated the book's pages.

"Oh we looked it up before we came," said V. "Fermentation, neglect, nature, death, etc. That should get us started. Let's start with The Rust Age."

Willie shook her head. V, she thought, was delighted. Willie wanted to run away. "This is not art I like," she thought. "This is not art. This is a drunken nightmare."

"I like 'an air of rotted elegance,' " said V, as they pulled themselves up the staircase, past paintings hung to the ceiling along the staircase walls. The paintings were bizarre, with dim figures, animals with tails and claws and protruding eyeballs, seaweed-like plants floating about creatures that were all teeth and scales. Some semi-human figures appeared, many half fish or crab, being eaten by their fellow other-worldly beings.

"Ugh," said Willie under her breath. She was breathing hard. She couldn't let V know how horrifying she found the space – the tightness of the aisles (they were in the upstairs by then) and the thick dust among the moss inside the fake aquariums, where creatures that never existed peeped out from behind warped trees and menacing ferns. Willie wanted out.

Willy looked at what V was gazing at. A mermaid-like sculpture occupied a central position inside the glass rectangle. It was sculpted out of dirt-filled clay, with suckers instead of hands. It was in the middle of creatures and matter that were both real and yet quite unreal, skeletons entwined in muddy straw and string stuck together with lumpy clay. The room also held dioramas, paintings, hideous metal and clay figures, unnatural creatures having unnatural sex.

"Can we go now?" said Willie. She groped her way back to the staircase.

"OK," said V. "I thought you might find it funny, but I guess…."

"I'm feeling sort of queer," said Willie. "I need some air. Maybe I'm allergic."

The two women made their way back down the stairs, and Willie scurried outside. V lingered. Willie heard her talking to the man behind the desk.

"Quite fantastic," V declared. "I love the surreal. Especially now."

Willie climbed into the car and drove V home, silent the whole way. She was not interested in big words about such terrible things. The two women parted, with nothing more than a civil "good by" and "thank you."

The zymoglyphic museum almost finished the Old Lady Adventures. The next time they met over mimosas, V tried to explain surrealism to Willie. She waxed eloquent about the phantasmagoric and the stuff of the unconscious. Willie was having nothing of it.

"I hated it, every single minute of it. I wanted to crush those monsters. I felt like my soul was being sucked into the mold."

"I didn't know you had a soul," said V. Willie got up to get coffee.

V glanced out the Monti windows. She was ashamed of having upset Willie. But Willie's insistence that V stop being depressed was irritating. And this museum made a new story for Conrad, who needed distractions. However, she wouldn't tell Conrad she had been snarky to Willie. Conrad would disapprove.

Then it was Willie's turn.

IV

"So," said V. "What's up for today?" V was aware she had offended Willie with the zymoglyphic muckery. She, V, had been feeling bullied, but now she felt guilty. Willie was trying to pull her back from depression and that was kind of her. But, she thought, Willie needed to know that the world was not all pretty flowers and tidy stories.

"I've made an appointment for 2 p.m.," said Willie. "We have just time enough for a mimosa."

The two women settled into their chairs at Monti's, wine glasses in hand. Two or three other café regulars stopped by the table to say hello. A younger woman (no older than 70, V thought) with dyed red hair and classy fingernails stopped to chat. A thin, sparkly older woman bounced up to the two of them and smiled broadly.

"You should have heard the gospel choir last week," she said to Willie.

Willie introduced her to V as Alyssa-The-Minister. An old gentleman came up behind Alyssa and handed her a cup of coffee. A tall, garishly dressed woman chattered at them as she walked by to join a gaggle of friends in the back. Willie knew them all. V was impressed by Willie's connections to the Monti's scene.

"Drink up, Darlin' ", said Willie. "We've got a date."

"Where to today?" asked V. "Oh my, we are going fancy, aren't we?"

Jake's Jeep Cherokee, parked along the curb, was pristine – seats that looked new, sparkling windows, no dirt on the floor mats. Willie said, "I thought we should go upscale today, more hoity-toity." She usually drove an old Honda Civic with foam coming out of its plastic seats. "We're going to Sellwood, down by Oaks Bottom."

The river was the Willamette, and Sellwood was an old leafy neighborhood with a big park along the water's edge.

"Sellwood, eh? A little hike around the swamp? A ride on the Ferris wheel at the Amusement Park?" said V.

V liked Sellwood. She and Conrad had walked trails in and around the big grassy park, and she and the young Caddie had spent summer days at the Oaks Bottom Amusement Park. In her 70s, she had painted scenes along the river, using the park benches to hold her equipment. It was a fine place to spend an afternoon, with lots of families and Frisbees and loping dogs.

“I didn’t wear my walking shoes,” said V. “I hope we aren’t hiking too far into the woods.”

“Oh no,” said Willie. “We aren’t going to the woods at all.” She smiled.

V was made uneasy by Willie’s cheer.

Willie pulled into a parking lot across from a sprawling set of Spanish-style buildings. A large sign said: “Parking for Portland Memorial Funeral Home. Mausoleum, Crematory, Funeral Home.”

“Oh God, Willie, what are we doing here? It’s a mortuary, for god’s sake. What are you saying – ‘Bring out your dead?’ ” said V.

“Not a mortuary,” said Willie. “A mausoleum. Although I looked it up, and it’s really part mausoleum and part ‘col-um-bar-ium’ – and also a mortuary.”

“A columbarium? Um, a death house?” V shuddered. She thought maybe they should have gone to the stripper bar.

“Well, yes, there’s that. Actually, though, it’s a Portland treasure, a whatchamacallem—a Heritage Thingie. Just wait. You’ll see.”

Inside the stuccoed pink building, it was all hard surfaces with a chilly air. The marble lobby area with dark wood had a stained glass ceiling through which the sun threw weird colors. The business offices were in discrete, separate rooms. Clicking heels could be heard from a distance, down an echoing hallway. Then a 40-some blonde woman appeared.

"You here for the tour?" the approaching woman said. "I understand someone has a loved one here, is that right? Would you like the tour first or to go directly to the resting place?"

There was nothing icky sweet about the woman's voice, although the language was specific to funeral homes. But, thought V, what choice did employees of such a place have?

"Oh I think a tour first," said Willie. "My friend here has never been inside the Wilhelm before. My husband's grandmother can wait another hour or so."

The blonde, relieved of her more funereal duties, turned on her tour guide voice. V only half listened.

"Hey," said Willie. "Nine miles of what? What did you say? That's crazy!"

"Nine miles of corridors," said the guide, "all marble, of course, although some have carpet. Ninety-seven thousand-plus folks have their final resting place here, so over the years additions to the original building were made. The buildings date from 1901 to the 1980s – lots of corridors and marble."

V shook her head. Ninety-seven thousand dead bodies here, in this cold, marble-and-stucco building.

"It's actually eight stories, with parts underground," the guide continued. "It got so big they had to use concrete for the later structures. The pink stucco is original, but there was a lot of demand. So the owners just added on and added on, especially to the back, down the hill toward the water."

"You can see the great blue heron mural from the other side of the river," added Willie, turning to V. "Maybe you saw that from the river trail on the west side? You said you hiked a lot

"The blue heron? The blue heron mural that flies over Oaks Bottom swamp -- near the Sellwood Bridge?" asked V.

"That's it." The guide and Willie spoke together.

"One side of the building was big and blank, so the Parks and Rec people convinced our owners to have a mural painted, and we became an even greater Portland treasure."

The tour felt endless to V. Lots less than 9 miles – they only went a little way into the building and used the tiny elevators – but they saw 12 or 15 stained glass windows – in the sickly yellow colors, V thought, of yesteryear. They saw chapels where V yearned to sit down, chapels done in gray and white marble, with black streaks. They saw bump-outs of small, fenced family rooms with interments of full-sized bodies as well as cremated remains. The drawers lining the corridors were wood, with marble surrounds. The air was dank. The more expensive rooms, with intricately curved, wrought-iron gates, were locked to protect the marble-encased remains. Un-cremated dead bodies were installed along the hallways' lower marble thirds. V had visions of stuffing bodies into dresser drawers. Cremated remains were placed in urns and vases in marble niches above them.

A Pieta, modeled on Michelangelo's original, graced one of the chapels. A marble version of the Last Supper fronted another. The few windows to the outside mostly showcased stained glass, but a couple of them looked out over Oaks Bottom, the wildlife refuge that teamed with blackbirds and tall browning weeds. Ducks moved across the open water and lifted themselves on translucent wings, flapping to soaring elegance. V stared out at the green and blue landscape. She longed to be there, in sunlight and air, anywhere but in this hushed, dank space.

Willie was chatting up the tour guide.

"Did you ever get locked in? Ever see a ghost?"

The tour guide laughed. "Nope, never saw or heard or even felt a ghost. We think they're content where they are – or maybe our locked drawers are too hard for them to get out of."

She continued, "I was never locked in, but once my boyfriend and I were having a pizza and beer downtown when an alarm went off. I had to come back here about 11 at night and turn it off. He and I figured we could rob a bank and the cops would never find us in here. I know every single door and side aisle and secret passage (used for maintenance, of course) – no one could ever find me if I didn't want to be found. Of course, the food offerings could be an issue."

The guide laughed and then looked a little abashed. She changed the subject, and turned to naming famous Portland leaders entombed within the walls.

"Does this corridor lead to the outside?" V interrupted her.

"Ah, um, yes – it's a side yard, but if you just go down there and turn left down the staircase, there's a door – unlocked for the yard guy...." The guide looked closely at V. "Are you OK?"

"I think I've had enough," V said, her voice choked. "Willie needs to check out that relative."

V had to get out, away from it all, especially Willie, who was now discussing scandals about various Portland grandees laid to rest in the columbarium. Willie called to V making her way down the corridor toward the door, but V dismissed her, waving her hand, pushing at her, so Willie turned back to the guide.

V opened a heavy door and found a marble bench, warm and sun lit, at the side of the pink stucco building. A heavy-set man was mowing the lawn. She was grateful for the lawnmower's roar. It smelled like new-mown grass and a slight tint of rot from the river. Trees lined the street across from the small side yard, and a mother and toddler wandered down the sidewalk. V breathed more easily.

"I think I had a panic attack," she said to herself. "I guess that was what it was. All that marble, crashing down, bodies everywhere, all those souls rising up through the dust."

V heard her cousin Nora's voice in her head. "Don't take on so. Don't be absurd."

"Stop the drama queen stuff!" V could hear Nora clearly. V's mother had a soft voice that seldom spoke to her from the grave, but Nora could always command her to "Settle down."

V fixed her eyes on the big maple across the street. She heard Willie open the door beside her.

V

The two women drove to V's house, where Caddie's car was parked along the curb. They walked along the path that meandered toward the back of the house, through small gardens. Each separate garden room had a distinctive feel; the colors and shapes of the foliage were varied and encased the walkways.

The path led to the studio at the back of the lot. V unlocked the door, and she and Willie went inside. They sat down in the worn studio chairs. The room was full of canvases, leaning against the walls, lying on tables, some half-finished, full of light and color. Rolling carts overflowed with painting equipment. Windows ran along the top of the walls, showing green leaves and dappled sun from the outside. The lower walls were covered with drawings and swatches of bright fabric and paper.

V checked her text messages and then looked up at Willie. "I like color," she said. Her voice was quiet. "And always too much. 'Over the top' as Conrad would say." She shrugged.

"I haven't painted in six months. That palette over there – laid it down on a Sunday, had the doctor's appointment on Monday, and there it sits. I can't imagine what I was thinking then, my fingers, the brush against the canvas. I killed those paint brushes, never cleaned them. Now they're useless." V slumped further into her chair.

Willie turned on the hot pot beside the muck-out sink. "I'll make us some tea. Or do you have coffee?" The two women had not spoken during the drive from Sellwood to the neighborhood. The tour had been cut short. Willie didn't visit Jake's grandmother.

"Here, this will put hair on your chest." Willie handed the cup to V. The tea had steeped longer than recommended. V sipped and grimaced.

"I'm sorry I took you to the Mausoleum," Willie said. "It didn't occur to me that it would be so personal. I'm just a klutz, a stupid klutz." Her voice dropped.

It was only the bite of the tea that kept V from snapping at Willie. Tea was brisk and fresh. And she was in her studio, and the paintings were evidence of the other days -- days when she had been brisk and fresh. Those days had existed.

The canvases, those adventures with Con, the evidence was all around.

"All these paintings have stories," said V. "I sat under that fir tree for a long time before I painted it. When I saw it with an old friend leaning against it, drinking beer. I added the figure. And that panorama? Diamond, Oregon, population 5, right-wing, red-neck country where all the cowboys drive up ranch roads and gaze out across the buttes to the cedar mountains. It's magical -- the atmosphere is luminous. And oh, the horses, the horses."

V remembered a rancher bringing her hand up to his horse's neck, the "softest thing" he ever felt. It was like the best sex V had ever had – the rancher's hard scratchy fingers pulling hers to the muscled neck of the restless creature, teaching her how to pull her fingers down over the fur, just enough to calm, not too much to stir the horse. That rancher must have been 80 years old, she thought, younger than I am now, but 20 years older than I was then. Sheer magic.

Willie sat down. "You were really upset at the mausoleum," she said. "Was it Conrad?"

"No, well, yes, probably," said V. "It was everything, really, I mean all the dead, of course, but worse. All that marble. It was so hard, so finished. It was absolutely perfectly aligned, every drawer, every urn, every black-gated room. All clean and cold."

"My house is a real mess," she continued. "Even the studio – the unwashed brushes, that open solvent tin -- and the house hasn't been dusted in months. I try not to run the dishwasher and hate it when I have to turn on the exhaust fan over the stove. It has to be quiet so he can sleep. And the mausoleum was so quiet, except for that tap-tap-tapping of the woman's heels …." V dropped her head into her hands and curled into herself.

This was the most V had ever said about her life at home with Conrad, as he lay, helpless, in bed. The gush of words followed by the balling up of her head and hands into her stomach – language and posture, as if all the supports that held her up had been withdrawn.

And then V raised her head and smiled, a real smile that reached her eyes. "Dear Willie, you turned me inside out. I think I hate you." She got up and reached under an open shelf and pulled out a bottle of wine.

"We need to drink to inversions," V said. "Souls, like weather, always in flux."

Willie found glasses beside the wine bottles and talked about her life, telling stories about traveling with various husbands. V talked about painting in the Petrified Forest and Montana in December. And then V looked at her phone and told Willie she had to go back to Conrad, that Caddie was about to leave. Willie reached over and pulled V toward her for a hug. V stiffened, then willed herself to soften, and Willie knew she was forgiven.

VI

Willie was nervous about seeing V again. She spent a week brooding about what she could do to ease V's pain.

V came in late that Wednesday – the café was almost empty. She got a mimosa and sat down with Willie, who was thumbing through a book on gardening. Willie had notions about removing her lawn and making it all flowers – she admired V's blooms – but Jake hadn't yet heard about Willie's plans.

V noted the book as soon as she sat down. "Oh, that old thing," she said. "Don't read it. You need to check out Ann Lovejoy; she's more fun."

Willie looked at her.

"How's Conrad?" she asked.

"Well," said V, slowly, "surprisingly better, we think. He's off chemo and gained a half pound and I got him to listen to *La Traviata* – well, the arias – the other night and he almost made it through the second act before he fell asleep."

Willie groaned silently. A man has prostate cancer and his wife is making him listen to opera?

"Yeah," said V, seeing Willie's frown. "I wondered if opera was a bit over the top, but I was yearning for some music and it's pretty nifty at first – drinking songs and romance and all that. I thought he needed something to take him out of himself. He's been scared – we've been scared – and maybe, I thought, he'd forget himself a bit."

"And the next morning I read him *The Times* while he had coffee and Cream of Wheat in bed, and he laughed at the political stories."

"You know, Willie," she said. "I decided I was a cold bitch, a person with no heart. I was taking care of Conrad like a robot. Doing all that had to be done but I couldn't love him. I mean, there was like ice or stone – a marble square where I thought love should be. I mean, I did it all – cooked and cleaned up, washed him, read to him, changed the sheets. I was always behind in the chores and all the time I was thinking that I was a monster, that I didn't really know what love was, that it couldn't be this, this mechanical thing, clicking through the house, marking off lists, making phone calls, doing research, talking to nurses and technicians and taking phone calls from our friends, being efficient and kind and overwhelmed. I could only do it if I didn't love."

"Geez," said Willie. "You OK, then? Breathing again?"

V looked at Willie.

"Yes." She said. "I did some meditation for the first time in months and the online guru just kept murmuring, 'breathe.' And I did and I got warm again."

Willie looked down at the table. "When Llewelyn died," she said, "I was a pile of jelly. A slime heap. A pile of, well, you know, poop. I stayed that way for a year and a half and then one day I looked at an old rock he had picked up off the desert floor. And I felt something in me taking shape, holding me up."

""The land will hold you up."" V said. "That's a line from a poem by Bill Stafford. He's from Oregon, you know."

The two women smiled at one another. They raised their coffee cups, gestured a toast, and drank.

VII

Over the next month, Conrad gained strength rapidly. One day Caddie drove him and V to Monti's. He was thin and pale and pleased to see Willie. Although he had never met her formally, he had come to love her because she was so good to V. And Willie was delighted to see him. She brought him a refill on his coffee when it got tepid, and V smiled at her and nodded.

V introduced Willie to Caddie. Willie shook Caddie's hand firmly and told her how good it was to be able to have spent such time with V, and how V had told her that Conrad was in good hands during those Wednesdays. She recounted how she had met V over a spilled mimosa and how their Old Lady Adventures had been a great way to get to know the city.

Caddie smiled and said she had checked out the Twin Pines Country Club, and indeed, the lemonade was very sweet. As were the children.

Then Caddie asked, "Have you ever seen the plane trees in Laurelhurst Park?"

Willie shook her head. "Plain trees?" she said, wondering what was important about just plain trees.

Caddie said, "London plane trees. They are really interesting. You two should check them out."

"Hey, V," said Willie. "Caddie thinks we should go to Laurelhurst and check out the – the what trees?"

V said, with an approving glance at Caddie: "Oh, the London planes – oh mercy, they are magnificent."

V went on. "The park has a lot of different areas -- but the grove, it's a big meadowy space with Oregon trees circling it – that's a world in itself. Humongous Doug firs are on the upper perimeter, behind the London Plane trees, and in front of the plane trees is an open meadow, all flowering weeds and field plants. It's a really nice space, but the plane trees are the jewels – like Tolkien's Ents. The trunks are massive -- their roots rise up out of the ground like enormous knees and big toes."

V spread her arms wide.

"You're a tree hugger!" said Willie. "Whoda thunk?"

Caddie said, "Laurelhurst Park is listed on the National Register of Historic Places. The trees are worth a special trip."

And so the last Old Ladies' Adventure checked out what V christened the Plane Tree Grove. The grove was at the western end of the park, a good distance away from heavily-used children's playground and tennis courts. The western end of the park was reserved for a semi-wilderness experience.

A paved path, running under firs, oak, cedar and sequoia trees, circled the outer edge of a large natural area. Other paths, lined in pine duff and ground plants, wandered down the slope toward an open center. These walkways curved through Oregon grape, juniper, nandina, and rhododendron. The air was soft and fragrant, and moss, neon green and viridian, lay on the rocks and smaller tree trunks. The shrubs thinned out and opened up near the bottom, where a large meadow lay, ringed by the plane trees.

Willie stepped into the meadow, looking across its open, sun-filled space. Lightly groomed grasses and flowers grew freely to meet the circling trees.

V, standing behind Willie, braced herself against the side of one of the plane trees. The bark of the enormous tree was rough against her fingers. V looked up the tree's length, seeing bulbous growths that flowed down the trunk. Higher up, sheets of bark hung like fabric off its upper trunk. Underneath the long lengths of loose bark V could see a creamy off-white layer of new growth.

V patted and then ran her fingers along the tree's dappled and bulging skin. The bark felt solid, ancient.

In the meantime, Willie had stepped into the open space, turned around once, and then again, looking first at the dark rim of trees behind her and then out to the wide blue sky. One arched cloud, with a ragged center, sat at the far side of the opening. The grass was dotted with feverfew daisies and tufts of dried milkweed, gone to silk.

Willie turned back to see V, leaning against the plane tree. She walked over to another, whose roots rose from the ground. Two of the roots formed a nook between them, one root being thigh high, the other a bit shorter. Willie lowered herself between the two tree arms. She wiggled her back side to fit into the hollow and laid her arms against the massive roots that surrounded her. She sighed with contentment.

V, moving carefully, sat down on the higher of the roots between which Willie had placed herself. She detected Willie's sweat-and-earth-toned fragrance.

"I can breathe here," said V. "Do you smell the pine trees?"

"Oh yeah," said Willie. "It smells good in a dusty kind of way. I see what you mean about these trees. This one is giving me a hug."

V laughed. "It's holding me up nicely too," she said, "even if I can't get my arms around it."

Willie responded. "The tree-hugger's dilemma," she said. "Trees that are too big to get your arms around."

Then, Willie added "It's a bit like life, I guess. Too big to get your arms around, even after all these years."

V said, "Back home – in Pennsylvania, I mean -- I used to sit just at the edge of woods, facing a meadow like this." And then she laughed: "And my pants always got dirty and damp and my mother knew where I'd been."

Willie said, "Ants in your pants?"

And V laughed out loud. "No ants in my pants now. I'm too old."

'Me too," said Willie. She looked up the tree trunk until her head couldn't tip back any more. She saw a creamy color under drapes of fluid bark and the large drooping globes, like soft breasts, extending down the trunk toward the two women. Willie felt a massive sense of ease and comfort, held close to the earth and the tree that reached into the sky.

V sighed. "There's nothing like this place, nothing except maybe being a baby again." She laughed at herself: "Too late for that," she snorted. "I'll take this."

The two women leaned into the massive tree. And then V stood up and said, "Time to go home." She reached down to help Willie out from between the roots. "Up you go, Missy," she said.

As Willie got to her feet, she leaned against V, who lost her balance and started to go sideways, her knee crumpling under her. Willie grabbed her and the two women held on to one another, steadying themselves as they regained stability.

"The land will hold us up," said V, again, "But sometimes it needs a little help from our friends."

Willie offered her bent elbow to V, and the two women walked to the path between the firs. It was uphill, but they went at a steady pace, their arms entwined for comfort and cheer. They were quiet, listening to the world they were rejoining.

ACKNOWLEDGEMENTS

Grateful acknowledgements to my zero draft, first draft, second draft, and third-plus draft readers, Jule Ward, Susan Saling, Jan Underwood and Jer Underwood, as well as the participants in my writing groups, Chris Gullion, Pat Sanders, Shelly Ballering, Diana Scholls, Linda Toenniessen and Martha Bosworth. All these trusted readers had brilliant insights, compassionate comments, and caught lots of excessive as well as missing commas.

I also need to thank the staff of Monti's Café, in Montavilla (Portland) Oregon, for being themselves. Without them, these stories couldn't have existed.

Special thanks to Jer, who rescued me when I most needed it.

ABOUT THE AUTHOR

June O Underwood is a visual artist and writer living in an old suburb of Portland, Oregon with her husband of 62 years. She is the author of *Sculpting the Mist: Reports from Elderhood 2019 – 2021*. Her visual art runs from quilted textiles through large oil canvases and hanging wire "thingies." *Wednesdays at Monti's* is her first book of short stories. She wishes to assure everyone that while the people depicted at the Café are imaginary, Monti's Café, in the little village of Montavilla, is thriving.

www.ingramcontent.com/pod-product-compliance
Lightning Source LLC
LaVergne TN
LVHW050627100826
845148LV00011B/1760

* 9 7 9 8 9 8 7 7 9 0 7 5 5 *